"Brady, I need to tell you something,"
Abigail began hesitantly. "I—"

He brought her tighter against him on the small dance floor. "You feel so good in my arms."

His voice floated around her, caressing her, just the way his green eyes had. *Tell him,* a voice whispered. But a louder voice said, *A little more time won't matter. Take this moment and hold on to it....*

He brought her hand to his chest and smoothed his thumb over her knuckles. "What did you want to tell me?"

His hand on her back was scorching through her sweater. His thumb on her hand was creating a rippling pleasure throughout her body. His shirt under her fingers, the scent of clean soap, his beard almost brushing her chin—all were intoxicating her.

"Nothing," she murmured. "Not now...."

Dear Reader,

Welcome to Silhouette **Special Edition**...welcome to romance.

In this festive month of December, curl up by the fire with romantic, heartwarming stories from some of your favorite authors!

Our THAT SPECIAL WOMAN! title for December is *For the Baby's Sake* by Christine Rimmer. Andrea McCreary's unborn baby needed a father, and her decision to marry friend Clay Barrett was strictly for the baby's sake. But soon, their marriage would mean much more to them both!

Lisa Jackson's LOVE LETTERS series continues this month with *C Is for Cowboy*. Loner Sloan Redhawk is hot on the trail of his prey—a headstrong, passionate woman he won't soon forget! Also returning to **Special Edition** in December is reader favorite Sherryl Woods with *One Step Away*.

Rounding out this holiday month are *Jake Ryker's Back in Town* by Jennifer Mikels, *Only St. Nick Knew* by Nikki Benjamin and *Abigail and Mistletoe* by Karen Rose Smith.

I hope this holiday season brings you happiness and joy, and that you enjoy this book and the stories to come. Happy holidays from all of us at Silhouette Books!

Sincerely,

Tara Gavin
Senior Editor

Please address questions and book requests to:
Silhouette Reader Service
U.S.: 3010 Walden Ave., P.O. Box 1325, Buffalo, NY 14269
Canadian: P.O. Box 609, Fort Erie, Ont. L2A 5X3

KAREN ROSE SMITH

ABIGAIL AND MISTLETOE

SPECIAL ✦ EDITION®

Published by Silhouette Books
America's Publisher of Contemporary Romance

To Linda Seidel, who gives her clients hope and a new image of themselves so they can face life again. To Linda's staff, especially Jennifer, who answered all my questions so patiently.
The Art of Corrective Makeup (Doubleday) by Linda Seidel with Irene Copeland was my source for technical information concerning trauma makeup artistry.

 SILHOUETTE BOOKS

ISBN 0-373-09930-4

ABIGAIL AND MISTLETOE

Books by Karen Rose Smith

Silhouette Special Edition

Abigail and Mistletoe #930

Previously published under the pseudonym Kari Sutherland

Silhouette Special Edition

Wish on the Moon #741

Silhouette Romance

Heartfire, Homefire #973

KAREN ROSE SMITH,

as a teenager, created scenes in her mind to fit popular songs. Those scenes developed into stories. Reading romances has been a favorite pastime throughout her life, and her love for the genre led her to apply the skills of her English degree to writing romances after back surgery. Now she can't imagine doing anything else. She says, "I try to write stories about hope and overcoming obstacles. My characters are as real to me as my friends. I share their pain as well as their joy and cheer them on as they resolve their conflicts."

Karen lives with her husband, Steve, son Ken, and cat, Kasie, in Hanover, Pennsylvania. She welcomes letters from readers.

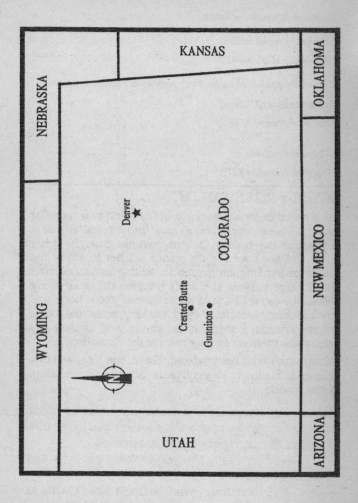

Chapter One

"I don't know why I let you talk me into this," Brady Crawford muttered as his black hiking boots purposefully ate up the distance between the parking lot and Colorado's Gunnison Airport terminal.

"Because you like to do favors for your old man," Ethan Crawford returned with a twitch of his lips that almost qualified as a smile.

Brady glanced at the man beside him as they kept step around the circular drive. At age sixty-five, his father was getting older, but was far from old. He was as vital and strong as he'd ever been. "A favor is one thing. Disrupting our peace is another. You know how I hate publicity, reporters and hangers-on."

"It wasn't too long ago you took the publicity and reporters in stride."

The stiff December wind buffeted Brady with as much force as his memories sometimes did. "That was nine years ago, Dad. I like the seclusion of the mountains, the guests who come to the lodge because they want quiet and solitude. Having a movie star there doesn't lend well to the atmosphere. Especially if she decides to promote the lodge to other movie stars.''

''Have you even heard a peep out of Theadora? She's been hiding in her cabin since she arrived yesterday.''

Brady's boot scrunched a snow mound on the walk. ''Yeah, well, this lady we're picking up today might change all that. I'm sure she's not meeting with Theadora out of the goodness of her heart. If she's a makeup artist, she probably wants to go places in Hollywood. Theadora might be simply a stepping stone for her.''

''Theadora's been a recluse for too long. If this Abigail Fox can get her to go out in public without her veil, I'll pay the woman's fee myself and introduce her to anyone in Hollywood I know.''

Brady knew his father's friendship with the world-famous Theadora Lorimar went way back. Once upon a time Ethan had been her chauffeur. When he began his own limousine service, he'd left her employ, but they'd remained friends. Theadora had never treated Ethan as a servant. Brady suspected his father felt more than friendship for Theadora but had never felt himself to be her equal.

Brady stuffed his gloved hands into his pockets. Theadora's accident had changed everything for the two old friends. For the past few years, ever since her accident, she'd refused to see Ethan when he wanted to fly back to Beverly Hills for a visit. She had cut herself off from everyone—until a few weeks ago, when she'd called and asked Ethan if they had a vacancy at the lodge for the holidays for her and a young woman who would try to teach her to cover her facial scars with makeup.

Brady knew about scars—emotional rather than physical ones. They were tough and stubborn and sometimes you could cover them up, but they never disappeared entirely. He was afraid Abigail Fox was more interested in making money and a name for herself than in helping Theadora. His years in Hollywood as a stuntman had taught him people had ulterior motives, not selflessness in mind.

Inside the terminal there was hustle and bustle—guests flying in to ski at Mount Crested Butte Resort, others to explore the quaint town of Crested Butte, students from Western College in Gunnison flying home for the holidays. Christmas didn't mean much to Brady now. It hadn't for a long time, even though he and his staff decorated the lodge, hung wreaths on the cabin doors and served an elegant Christmas dinner. He supervised the activities; he didn't get involved in them.

Flipping his sunglasses to the top of his head, he checked his watch and then the arrival time on the board for Abigail Fox's flight from Texas. He headed toward the gate, his father beside him. "You didn't have to come to town with me today. I could have picked up the supplies and Ms. Fox myself."

Ethan lifted his black Stetson from his head and ran his hand through his gray hair. "I wanted to spend time with Theadora. But with that damn veil between us..." He paused and shook his head. "I haven't seen her for three years and she *still* won't let me see her." Replacing his hat and shrugging, he concluded, "You can always use a hand with those cartons of canned goods. Truth is, I didn't want to give you the chance to chase Ms. Fox away.''

"I wouldn't do that. This means too much to you and Theadora.''

"To Theadora,'' Ethan corrected.

Brady shook his head. Stubborn. Like father, like son. Ethan had convinced himself long ago that he and Theadora could never be more than friends. Just as Brady had convinced himself that Pine Hollow Lodge on the outskirts of Crested Butte was where he belonged.

Passengers were disembarking as he and his father reached the waiting area. Brady didn't know what to expect, but when he saw the woman coming toward him, he didn't have any doubt as to who Abigail Fox was.

The deep purple coat trimmed in turquoise was too elegant for the Gunnison Airport where jeans and ski parkas were normal sights. Her silk-clad legs were long with curves that made his gut clench until he got to her feet; then he almost burst out laughing. *Spiked heels*.

He hadn't seen spiked heels on a woman in years. Even Theadora had had the good sense to wear sturdy boots. His grin almost turned into a rumble of laughter when he realized Ms. Fox was struggling with a garment bag over her left shoulder, a large suitcase in her right hand and a rectangular case the size of a weekender in her left. The garment bag's strap had slipped down her arm.

Closing the distance between them in a few long strides, he reached for the large suitcase. "Let me take that for you.''

She'd been shifting her luggage on his first perusal, and her head had been bowed. Now, she lifted her gaze to his. Her eyes were the most beautiful shade of blue. He'd seen wildflowers that color when he'd gone hiking in the summer. Her hair was a combination of burnished copper and amber. It wasn't curly, but waved around her face as if it was caressing her, and then fell to her shoulders. She wasn't model-beautiful, but something about her eyes drew his to them again. There was a gentleness there, or was it vulnerability? Or maybe it was a shadow of something running too deep to be named.

Then she blinked, and he relegated his analysis to sheer whimsy. Her lips lifted in a tentative smile. ''Mr. Crawford?''

Her smile put a dimple at both corners of her mouth—a very lovely mouth. Brady's stomach clenched again and the desire to return her smile burned into desire of another kind. He simply nodded and reached for her suitcase. ''I'll take that for you.'' As he lifted it, he could feel her gaze on him and he looked up.

Caught looking, she admitted with a shy smile, ''I expected someone older. Miss Lorimar said . . .''

Brady gestured toward his father standing a few feet away. Ethan walked toward them with a grin and a twinkle in his gray eyes. He extended his hand to her. ''Ethan Crawford. This is my son, Brady. We're partners.''

''I'm pleased to meet you, Mr. Crawford.''

''Ethan. We don't stand on formality at Pine Hollow.''

''She's not going to stand at all if she doesn't ditch those shoes. I'll have to carry her to the Jeep.''

Abigail Fox looked taken aback for a moment, but then her chin lifted and defiance lit her eyes. The frost in her voice nipped his nose. "My boots are in the bottom of my garment bag, Mr. Crawford. I had a business appointment before my flight and dressed accordingly. In case you're interested, I also have a ski outfit, cords and sweaters in my suitcase, so I'm prepared for a Colorado Christmas."

Brady couldn't remember the last time someone had stood up to him and scored points. He should be mildly embarrassed or at least annoyed, but he wasn't. He felt the urge to smile and tried to suppress it. "What about long underwear?"

Abigail felt the heat crawl up her neck. She didn't let go of her temper like that, not usually. But she was tired, downright weary of five years of a nonstop pace that was her own choosing. She'd come to Pine Hollow Lodge, not only to help Theadora Lorimar but to take a much-needed vacation. She hadn't counted on running smack-dab into an attractive, black-bearded mountain man with green eyes as deep and stormy as an angry sea.

Noticing the slight twitch of his lips under his mustache, she answered, "Long underwear, too. Must you know the color for me to pass inspection?" His thorough appraisal as she'd struggled with her luggage had made her wish she'd sent everything ahead so she could make a more poised first impression. But then, why should she care what *he* thought of her? And if he had problems with her while her makeup was *on* . . . She brushed away the thought. It was old history.

Ignoring Brady Crawford and his piercing green eyes that seemed to accuse her of something, she made her way to a row of seats nearby and set down her makeup case. Plopping the garment bag on one of the chairs, she tried to unzip it. The zipper stuck. Before she could work with it, Brady was leaning over her, maneuvering the tab to investigate the problem.

She tapped his shoulder, but he merely arched his brows as the zipper slid smoothly down its track. She opened her mouth to tell him she was perfectly capable of unzipping her own garment bag, but witnessing his penetrating let's-just-get-your-boots-on-and-get-out-of-here look, she closed it again. She probably wouldn't be seeing much of Brady Crawford, so why make anything an issue?

"Never mind," she murmured as she reached into the garment bag and pulled out her tall, black leather, fur-lined boots. Paired up with wool socks, they would keep her as warm as she needed to be.

As she slipped off her pumps and took hold of one of the boots, Brady said to Ethan, "I'll go bring the Jeep to the door."

"That's not necessary—"

"Those leather soles won't give you much traction on an icy pavement. I want to get you to Pine Hollow in one piece." With a last look at her silk-stocking-clad foot, he turned and strode to the door.

Abigail hazarded a glance at Ethan. "Is he always so...impatient?"

Amusement glimmered in the older man's eyes. "Not ordinarily." He took a deep exaggerated breath. "Must be something in the air."

The only thing she smelled was the faint scent of her own perfume. She looked at the older man, perplexed, but he just smiled enigmatically.

Abigail didn't pay much attention to the route that led to Crested Butte, even though the scenery was snow-clad and postcard perfect. She was more concerned with keeping her body an inch from Brady's.

That was about all the spare room the Jeep afforded with her wedged between Ethan and his uncommunicative son. The back of the vehicle was loaded with cartons and sacks and a large ice chest.

Brady's elbow brushed her arm as he made a right turn. Her body instantly came to attention. The man was too big, too virile and too commanding to ignore. But she did her best as she struck up a conversation with Ethan about the history behind the mining town of Crested Butte.

A half hour later, Brady veered off the main route onto a snow-packed road. As the Jeep bumped over a rut, Abigail was jostled against Brady. His thigh was hard and taut against hers, his sheepskin jacket rough against the smooth wool of her coat. She caught a scent of soap or shampoo and wondered what kind of chin he hid behind that beard. Determined and set, no doubt. In profile, his bone structure was the same as his father's. But with his coal-black hair and beard, his green eyes rather than gray and the additional inch or two that brought him to at least six-foot-two or three, the resemblance was hard to see.

Beards had always intrigued her. While women used makeup so they could face the world, feel better about themselves and cover imperfections, men often grew beards to retreat, to barricade, to hide the essence of who they were. Was Brady Crawford hiding something?

Probably not. He probably wore it so he didn't have to shave. It could be as simple as that.

The bumpy road knocked her against him again, and she levered herself closer to Ethan. Brady glanced at her, but his sunglasses hid his eyes the same way his beard camouflaged his expression.

Evergreens heavy with snow lined the winding drive and after about a quarter of a mile, Brady pulled up in front of the lodge. Ethan took Abigail's hand to help her from the vehicle. In a low voice, he warned, "Be careful on the steps. They need another dose of calcium chloride."

She smiled. "Thanks." She had no doubt that if she slipped once, Brady would lug her over his shoulder and carry her inside. The thought caused a ripple of excitement to sweep through her, and she sucked in a breath of piercingly cold air. Truthfully, she hadn't thought of putting her hiking boots in the garment bag rather than her high boots. Apparently around here, practicality was all-important. She'd presumed Theadora Lorimar would have selected a luxury resort, and icy paths wouldn't be a consideration.

"Disappointed?" Brady asked as he came up beside her and saw her examining the lodge.

Abigail's gaze slipped over the three-story, cedar-sided lodge with its double gables and rough-hewn allure. "No. I didn't know what to expect. Miss Lorimar mentioned individual cabins...."

"They're out back. Theadora's in cabin five."

Ethan called to Brady. "I'll take the Jeep around to the kitchen to unload. You can get the lady settled."

Brady frowned and bent to pick up her luggage. She went for the makeup case at the same time he did and their hands brushed. He'd taken off his gloves in the car; she hadn't. The tight turquoise leather on her palm was practically a second skin and his large knuckles slid under the hollow of her fingers. Awareness of him skipped up her spine. Why? Probably because he was big and male and an unknown quantity.

Squaring her shoulders against the flash of attraction she felt, she said, "I can get it."

Brady ignored her words and firmly took hold of the weekender, easily lifting the other two pieces of luggage. With a quick glance at her boots, he said briskly, "Just get yourself inside safely. The railing should help."

He waited for Abigail to climb the steps. She did so carefully and breathed a sigh of relief as Brady held the door for her and she entered the lodge.

The outside appearance hadn't prepared her for the quality inside. Beautiful pine paneling and pine plank flooring gave the interior a warm, supremely rustic appeal. To the right, hand-hewn logs supported the vaulted ceiling of the great room, where she supposed guests gathered to socialize. Bookshelves framed a two-story native-rock fireplace with a low-burning fire. The furniture, grouped in curliquing circles, was teal green, the same color as the sheer curtains at the long ice-frosted windows. Tables for games or snacks were a multishaded oak. She couldn't see through the sheer panels of teal at the French doors, but suspected they led to a porch of some type.

Brady went to the reception desk and set down her luggage. She crossed to the desk as he flipped around a large guest book. Taking a key from inside a desk drawer, he said, "You're in room 140. The dining room is located down that flight of steps—"

"I'm in the lodge?"

He studied her cautiously. "Is that a problem?"

"You said Miss Lorimar is in cabin five. I'd like to be closer to her."

"I'll just bet you would," he muttered.

"Excuse me?"

He shook his head. "Theodora requested the farthest cabin from the lodge. I figured it would be more convenient for you...."

Her tone became firm and professional. "It would be more convenient for me to be near my client. Is that a problem?"

"This time of the season it is. We're full."

Abigail's gaze didn't waver from his. "I need to be close to her."

"Why?"

"I don't see that that's any of your business. I'm a paying customer and I prefer—"

"You're paying?" he asked dryly. "That's not what I heard. Theodora said to put your stay on her tab."

"Well, I'm telling you it doesn't go on her tab."

Brady narrowed his eyes as if trying to see her more clearly. After a penetrating pause, he said, "All right. I do have a cabin we just repaired. But the varnish on the woodwork is barely dry, and this one doesn't have a phone. You'll be cut off from the rest of the guests."

"Why did the cabin have to be repaired?" If the roof leaked or something like that...

Brady sighed. "One of our guests had a party in his cabin that got out of hand. Needless to say, he won't be a repeat customer. That's all I can offer you besides the lodge room."

"The cabin will be fine," she assured him with a note of fatigue she couldn't quite control.

"You're sure? When you're there alone at night and the outside darkness isn't even lit by the moon..." His voice trailed off, and she imagined the isolated picture he was trying to paint.

"Do you have a baseball bat?"

"What?"

She rolled her eyes. "I was kidding. I'll be fine."

His skeptical glower and another thorough once-over told her he didn't believe her. Brady Crawford definitely had a chip on his shoulder where she was concerned. Why?

He nodded toward the dining room. "Let's go that way."

She followed him down the steps and along a corridor that led to a spacious room with the same paneling as the reception area. The round tables were covered with Christmas-red cloths that held a square white tablecloth layered on top. Boughs of pine tied with red velvet ribbon adorned the walls. She'd noted the giant wreath at least four feet across in the reception area.

"Do you mostly have families booked at Christmas?"

Brady opened the door at the back of the dining room. "No. Families usually want an activity-oriented Christmas so they go to Crested Butte or to their resort, where there's skiing, shopping, social directors for the kids. All we have here is peace, quiet and a cross-country track."

"You do? That's wonderful. I've only tried it a few times. Can I rent skis?"

He closed the door behind them. "You don't have to rent them. But if you go, we have one rule. Don't ever ski alone."

Before she could assure him she'd keep his rules, he'd flipped on his sunglasses and started up the snow-packed path before them. Unfortunately, she couldn't follow suit—her sunglasses were in the pocket of her weekender, which carried all the supplies she would need to help Theodora Lorimar.

Brady's long legs moved him faster than she could manage. Every once in a while, he glanced over his shoulder. She couldn't tell if his attitude was protective or disgruntled.

They passed four cabins nestled in the pines, a good quarter acre apart. She began breathing heavier and her head pounded, but she figured she was just tired from the trip itself, as well as the hectic pace she'd maintained before the trip that would enable her to get away for a few weeks.

Finally, at a fork in the path, Brady motioned to the left. "There's Theadora's cabin." He took off again to the right. After what had to have been the equivalent of a good city block, she saw hers. All of the cabins thus far had been cedar-sided like the lodge. Hers was no different. Brady set down the luggage at the door.

While Abigail caught her breath, she looked around. At first glance, it seemed the path stopped at her cabin, but then she saw the boot prints. Moving to the side of the cabin so she could see around it, she spied not another cabin, but a house. A log house. "Who lives back there?"

"I do." He opened the cabin door, gathered her luggage and went inside.

Curious about the house, but more eager to get settled, Abigail followed him. The temperature inside the cabin was chilly, and the interior was almost . . . bare.

Brady went to the thermostat and turned it up. "I only kept it warm enough so the pipes wouldn't freeze. Sure this is where you want to stay?"

The compact kitchen consisted of an electric range, no oven, a small refrigerator and a few cabinets. The small counter was spruce green, the sink stainless steel, the refrigerator almond-colored. Beyond the kitchen was a doorway. She investigated, finding a bedroom with a double bed, a nightstand and a small chest with a mirror hung above it. The smell of fresh varnish lingered in the air.

"Well, is it this or the lodge?" he repeated.

Abigail preferred people. She didn't like isolation; she'd had enough of that as a child. But her first concern was her client. If Theadora Lorimar wanted to talk, as many of Abigail's clients did, she didn't want to be as far away as the lodge. "Is that a real fireplace?"

"This isn't a Hollywood stage set, Ms. Fox. There's firewood alongside the cabin. And in about fifteen minutes you'll be able to take off your coat."

"Then this will be fine."

He seemed surprised. "You're sure?"

"Mr. Crawford, I've made my decision. I like the cabin, though it is a little sparse. Do you think I could find a chair someplace?"

She wasn't sure, but a dark flush seemed to creep into his cheeks. "I told you we just finished repairs. I have the sofa, chair and table at my house. I'll bring them over as soon as I help Dad unload the supplies."

"Thank you."

He avoided her gaze. "Where would you like your luggage?"

"I'll take care of it."

He didn't argue. "If you need anything..."

"I'll go to the nearest cabin door or the lodge. Don't worry, I won't bother you."

His green eyes darkened and he frowned. "Go to Theadora if you need something. Don't go knocking on strange cabin doors."

"Who's in cabin four?"

"A businessman from the East Coast. He comes here because he wants the privacy."

"I see." She didn't really. She didn't understand the gruffness in Brady's tone.

Brady checked his watch. "Will you be here in an hour or so?"

She would like to unpack, but she wanted to see her client first. "Probably not. I'm going to try to catch Miss Lorimar."

"That shouldn't be too difficult. She hasn't made a move from her cabin since she arrived."

Something in his voice alerted her that he and Theadora Lorimar weren't strangers. "Do you know her?"

Again, his reaction was one of those Brady Crawford stares that seemed to bore right through her. "She and my father have been friends for a long time."

That didn't answer her question, but then she wasn't surprised. She didn't imagine Brady answered to anyone. "Does your father live with you?"

"No. He has an apartment on the second floor of the lodge," Brady answered, moving toward the door. "Do you plan to start a fire tonight?"

"I'd like to."

"I'll bring in some wood."

"You don't have to..."

He ducked through the door, effectively cutting Abigail's protest. Unbuttoning her coat, she took it off and threw it over the bed. Taking her barrette from her hair, she ran her fingers through it and rubbed at her temple, where the headache still pounded, though not as badly.

She heard Brady shut the door. When she stepped into the living room, he was already positioning kindling on the grate.

"I know how to build a fire. My brother taught me."

Brady didn't turn around, but laid three logs on top of the kindling. "Good. Then you'll know how to keep it going. Just be sure..." As he stood and turned toward her, his voice trailed off.

She nervously adjusted the wide turquoise leather belt cinching the waist of her deep purple suede-silk dress. His scrutiny unsettled her, making her feel gauche and sixteen again. She had the distinct urge to touch her cheek, but kept her hand by her side.

He quickly raked his hand through his hair. "Uh, just be sure the fire's out when you go to bed."

"I will." Her soft answer made Brady frown. His face was too lean, though the beard hid much of it. The grooves in his cheeks when he frowned cut deep, which led her to wonder if he frowned too much. Would they be just as deep when he smiled? Could she make him smile? More important, why did she want to?

He cleared his throat, took his sunglasses from the top of his head and headed for the door. "I have a key to the cabin. If you're not here, I'll bring the furniture in anyway, if that's all right with you."

She nodded. The next thing she knew, he'd closed the door behind him.

Abigail knocked on the door of cabin five and called, "Miss Lorimar? It's Abigail Fox."

After a minute or so, the door opened about two inches, then a few more. "I've been waiting for you.

Actually, I've been thinking since I arrived, and I'm not sure I want to go through with this."

Just getting a dark glimpse of Theadora's hat and veil, Abigail knew the most important thing to do at this point was to assure the actress she understood. "Could we discuss this, Miss Lorimar? You and I didn't come all this way to dismiss the idea without talking about it."

The actress opened the door so Abigail could step inside. She took a quick look around the cabin. It was exactly like hers, except that the counter and furniture were a cheery but subdued cranberry. A book lay open on the sofa and Abigail gravitated toward it. "*A Tale of Two Cities*. I see you're taking advantage of the quiet to do some serious reading."

"My life is serious now, Ms. Fox. I can't quite handle comedies anymore. They require hope."

"Call me Abigail. Do you mind if I sit down?"

"I'm sorry. Since the accident, my manners have changed along with my attitude."

Abigail placed the book on the coffee table, hoping the actress would sit beside her. She didn't. She kept her distance and lighted on the edge of the cushioned chair. She was a small woman, about five foot three, dainty in her high-necked, lace-edged, pastel pink sweater and matching wool slacks. The white felt derbylike hat with its shimmery white veil hid her face entirely. Her ash-blond hair was pulled into a chignon at her nape.

"Miss Lorimar—"

"Theadora."

Abigail nodded. "Theadora. On the phone, you told me you were tired of plastic surgery and afraid to try it again. I understand your skin has a tendency to scar.''

''I imagine some women could face the world as I am now. But I can't. For forty-five years my reputation as an actress, as a woman, as a person, has depended on my beauty. How can I possibly let my public see me like this?'' Her hands fluttered with agitation. ''I can't and I won't.''

''Are you saying you won't take off your veil unless you can look perfect?''

''*Perfect*. Intriguing word, isn't it? I never thought I was perfect. I had a mole here, a freckle there. And when the wrinkles started I thought about a face-lift, but everyone told me I was aging gracefully and still beautiful. Well, now I realize that before the accident I *was* beautiful, but now I'm not.''

''I can't evaluate what I can do for you unless I see you.''

''No one sees me, Abigail. Absolutely no one.''

''That must make you feel lonely.''

Theadora bowed her head. Her voice caught when she confessed, ''Very lonely.''

''You read the pamphlet and book I sent you?''

The older woman didn't answer directly. ''Since the last surgery failed, I'm afraid to hope that you can really work magic.''

''It's not magic, Theadora. I use color and illusion, shadows and light. And the result can be amazing, but not magic. But as I said, I have to see you to determine how much difference I can make.''

''I'm not ready for that.''

Abigail knew better than to press too hard, but she also knew to encourage. ''You're here, so maybe you are. However, I understand if you want to spend some time talking, asking questions, getting to know a little about me. We can do that."

Theadora leaned forward. "But you said this is your vacation. And your fee..."

"My fee covers whatever my client needs. I'll have plenty of time to do some skiing, work a little, enjoy the holiday and answer any questions you may have. I'm in cabin six. Unfortunately, I don't have a phone. Have you been going to the lodge for meals?"

Theadora retreated again and sat back against the chair. "Ethan has been bringing them to me."

"Brady said you and his father have been friends a long time."

"Yes. About forty years. Amazing, isn't it, how time passes? He was my first chauffeur. I had just made it, bought my first house in Beverly Hills. We've seen each other through some hard times. His wife passing on...Brady was only twelve. Ethan's done a magnificent job with that boy. He's had his share of hard times, too." She stared out the window into the snow-topped forest. "At my age, I have to wonder if my career has been worth everything I've given up. And now..."

"Theadora, life can be good again."

From the tilt of the actress's head, Abigail could tell the woman was studying her. Finally she said, "I wish I could believe that."

Brady switched off the ignition of the snowmobile in front of Abigail's cabin and jumped off as the late-afternoon sun played through the trees. When he rapped on the door, she didn't answer and he breathed a sigh of relief. Opening the door, he let it stand wide so he could bring in the furniture strapped on the snowmobile's trailer.

Untying the table lodged on the sofa, he hefted it up and carried it to the living room area. When he passed the bedroom doorway, he stopped short and slowly set the table on the floor.

Abigail Fox was stretched out on the bed on top of the blanket. The dress that had molded to each of her curves so lovingly had ridden up until it grazed her thighs. She was flat on her back, one curvy leg crossed over the other, her face turned to the right, her coppery hair fanning out to the left.

He took a step forward and stopped when the urge to touch her matched the fierceness of his body's response to her loveliness. He bet she had never expected to fall asleep. He bet she'd only intended to close her eyes for a few moments. He bet he'd better get out of the cabin fast before she caught him watching her.

When he'd left her cabin earlier, he'd been aroused as he hadn't been in years. He grimaced. He should be grateful to Abigail Fox because she'd broken the shell he'd wrapped around his mind, his premise that he didn't need a woman even for physical release. But he wasn't grateful. He was uncomfortable, unsettled and angry that she'd intruded into his hermitlike life—

Abigail sighed and turned her head.

Brady stepped back and held his breath. She didn't awaken. Restless, telling himself she was just another woman—and one with an agenda at that—he went to get the rest of the furniture, trying to forget how delicate and vulnerable Abigail Fox looked as she slept.

Chapter Two

Abigail woke to a loud *thunk* beyond her bedroom. Startled, she sat up and pushed her hair away from her face. Brady. It had to be...with her furniture. Her hand automatically went to her cheek, though intellectually she knew her makeup would still be as smooth and set as when she put it on that morning. It had been created to last, to look *more* natural than ordinary makeup, to be reliable, to give a sense of security to the wearer. But she couldn't help glancing in the mirror after she slid from the bed. Her reflected image told her everything was fine except for her mussed hair. Glancing at her watch, she saw she'd been asleep for about an hour.

The plank floor was chilly as she stepped into the living room, where Brady was fitting a shade to the floor lamp. His expression didn't tell her whether her sudden appearance was expected or unexpected. The slight lift of a brow was his only acknowledgment. She supposed he hadn't even looked into the bedroom, presuming she was with Theadora. Apparently she'd been sleeping too soundly to hear him knock.

He plugged in the lamp and switched it on. "Now you'll have a light to read by." His voice was deep and husky, and she had the strangest urge to invite him to take off his coat and sit down so she could find out more about him. The voice of caution inside her whispered, *Why? You know nothing can come of it.*

Still, she approached him anyway. "Could I get a few tea bags from your kitchen until I can do some shopping? I'd like to—"

"I'll be right back."

Abigail frowned. Had he heard her or was he ignoring her attempt at conversation?

In a few moments he was back with a basket in his arms. He set it on the coffee table. "This should take care of whatever you need for now. It's complimentary. It was in your room at the lodge."

The basket was a beautiful rusty wicker, piled high and wrapped with green cellophane. She untied the red ribbon and found an assortment of flavored teas, hot chocolate, cheese, crackers and summer sausage, as well as a bottle of sparkling grape juice and three bottles of mineral water. "This is lovely. Thank you."

He shrugged. "It's something we do for our guests." Crossing to the door, he added, "Dinner will be served from six-thirty until nine. The floodlights outside stay lit until eleven so you won't have to walk back in the dark."

"Theadora said she's been taking her meals at her cabin."

"We can provide that service if you'd like."

"No, I don't want it. Spending all my time alone isn't my idea of a holiday. But I did wonder if I could get Theadora to the dining room if there weren't too many people around. What time is breakfast?"

"Seven to nine. But you'd be better off trying to get her to lunch. We have a big crowd at breakfast, then guests scatter for the day." His eyes traveled up and down Abigail from her head to her toes. "I wish you luck. Even my dad hasn't been able to get her out of that cabin."

Abigail curled her toes as her feet got colder, but the rest of her heated up. Pulling out the box of hot chocolate packets from the basket, she asked, "Would you like something to warm you before you go out again?"

He studied her carefully, assessing her and the invitation. "Sorry. I don't have time to socialize." Opening the door, he said, "If you find you need anything, leave a note at the desk and we'll take care of it. Have a pleasant stay."

Rehearsed, recited and finished. With her murmured thank-you, Brady was out the door.

What had prodded her to ask him to stay? She shrugged. If Brady Crawford wanted to be polite rather than friendly, that was his prerogative. She would find some people she could talk to at dinner tonight and maybe ski with, and then she'd have another go at Theadora.

Before dinner that evening, Abigail went down the stairs to the lodge's lower level. The receptionist at the desk had told her the skis and equipment were located in the first room on the right. She heard noise before she found the room. Scuffling. Grunting. A smack. The scrape of furniture across the floor. A heavy thump.

Hurrying along the corridor, she saw the open door, hesitated momentarily, then went in. And quickly backed out again. Brady was fighting! Fistfighting. With a young man who couldn't be more than sixteen.

At her horrified sound of protest, Brady turned toward her, his broad shoulders in a red-and-blue flannel shirt seeming to take up much of the room. Just then, the teenager threw a hard punch and caught the edge of Brady's jaw.

Brady jumped back and swore.

The teenager, wide-eyed and openmouthed, froze. Then he apologized. "Brady. I'm sorry. I thought you were ready. Are you okay?"

Brady rubbed his jaw with a rueful glare at Abigail. "It's okay, Luke. Stray punches happen. If you want to be a stuntman you'll have to get used to bumps and bruises. But you *do* try to prevent as many as you can."

"A stuntman?" Abigail still didn't know exactly what was going on, but it wasn't a fight. That was now obvious.

Brady waved his arm toward Abigail. "Luke Underwood, Abigail Fox. She's a guest at Pine Hollow."

Luke stared down at his shoes and mumbled, "H'llo, ma'am."

Abigail smiled and extended her hand. "Hello, Luke. I thought you were in mortal danger." If Brady wouldn't tell her what was going on, maybe the teenager would.

The boy shook her hand and quickly released it. "Nah. Brady and me were practicing. I want to be a stuntman and since he's an expert, he's teachin' me." Luke looked at Brady with worshipful eyes. "He's the best."

Brady Crawford was a stuntman? And he was teaching this boy how to put himself in danger, to possibly damage himself for life? "I see. You're a stuntman, Mr. Crawford?"

Brady heard the disapproval in her voice, so opposite of her friendliness yesterday when she'd asked him to stay for a cup of hot chocolate. He'd been tempted. Lord, had he been tempted. She'd come out of that bedroom looking more delectable than any woman he'd ever seen. That was why he'd left.

"I used to be a stuntman."

Luke said to Brady, "I'd better go. Sheila's cookin' supper, and if I'm not there on time, Dad'll have a fit."

"Make an effort, Luke."

The teenager screwed up his face distastefully. "Yeah. Right." He rolled down his shirtsleeves. "I'll be over tomorrow to chop that wood." With a shy smile at Abigail, he left.

Brady was aware of Abigail's eyes on him, studying him, sweeping over his physique. It felt strange having her gaze on him—and arousing as hell. Shoving a table back into place that had been moved for his mock fight with Luke, Brady asked, "So what do you need?"

"I'd like to try your cross-country track tomorrow so I thought I'd look at the skis."

He motioned to the rack at the back wall. "Help yourself. The boots are in the cupboard underneath.

What size are you?'' He'd guess about a six. A perfect six.

"Six."

He smiled. "Try the skis on the left, second pair in."

Abigail crossed to the rack and took one of the skis down. She ran her hand over the fiberglass. "Why are you teaching Luke stunts?"

"Because he has energy to burn."

"Chopping wood doesn't do it?"

"I don't know about females, but males that age need more than odd jobs, especially when they're angry and frustrated."

Abigail examined the raised diamond patterns on the bottom of the touring ski. "What's Luke angry and frustrated about?"

Brady was surprised she asked. Why should she care about a boy she didn't know? "It's complicated."

Abigail propped the ski on the floor and raised her arm above her head to measure its length. The top of the ski reached her wrist. "Sorry. I'm used to asking questions of my clients. It's a habit."

The pair of skis was the right size for Abigail, as Brady had suspected. Suddenly he decided there wouldn't be any harm telling her about Luke. Depending on how long she stayed, she would probably see the teenager around. "Luke's mom died five years ago. His father started dating about a year ago and is engaged now. The last thing Luke wants is a stepmother. He wants freedom and a one-way ticket out of Crested Butte so he can 'see the world.' His words, not mine."

Abigail's gaze met Brady's, filled with compassion. "Adolescence is tough under the best of circumstances."

The depth of emotion in Abigail's eyes surprised him. Had her adolescence been so tough? He ignored the question as well as Abigail's appeal. "Luke's at that age when he wants more than he can ever have and thinks he can get it."

Abigail didn't say anything right away. She had a way of studying him that urged Brady to explain himself, which was strange. He hadn't felt the need to explain anything to anyone in the past few years.

Rubbing her hand over the ski again as if appreciating its quality, she finally said, "If we don't dream of more than we can achieve, we would never achieve as much."

"And what happens when the dreams are shattered and we don't want to dream again?"

"I can't live without dreaming," she said softly. "Can you?"

He had thought he'd stopped dreaming. He had thought he'd accepted a life that *he'd* chosen—one with guilt, but without emotional ties, without pain. But standing here with Abigail Fox, dreams he'd forced into the shadows peeked into the light. One very explicit dream at the moment. He didn't even know this woman. So why was she getting to him?

"Dreams are a luxury for some people," he responded tersely.

"But what about you?"

She'd taken this discussion from the hypothetical to the intensely personal much too fast. "Do your clients answer nosy questions?"

A smile tickled the corner of her mouth. "Eventually."

He shrugged. "I'm not your client." Again that appraising, curious look that almost made him want to apologize for his rudeness. Almost.

Then she turned and put the ski back on the rack. Opening the cupboard, she pulled out a pair of boots. She looked them over, and checked the size, pinching them between her fingers, and then closing the cupboard door with her knee.

Brady nodded toward the skis. "I'll carry them upstairs for you."

"That's not necessary. What I *would* like is a suggestion for a skiing partner for tomorrow. I can't find anyone who's interested."

"That's unusual. Usually someone wants to ski."

"Many of your guests are going Christmas shopping in Gunnison if they're not skiing the trails at Crested Butte."

"You're not interested in Christmas shopping?"

"I took care of that before I left Houston. Most of my presents had to be sent."

"You don't have family nearby?"

"No. My family's back East."

"You don't usually spend Christmas with them?"

"They're not all at the same place."

"Most people like to spend Christmas with people they care about."

"I care about my clients, Mr. Crawford. That's why I'm here."

Right. She cared about one very well-known client. "If you can't find someone at dinner tonight who'd like to ski tomorrow, leave a note at the desk for me. My father or I will show you the trail."

Her smile bloomed full and wide. "Guaranteeing customer satisfaction at Pine Hollow?"

"You could put it that way."

Hefting the skis over her shoulder, she crossed to the door. "Do you ever eat dinner with the guests?"

"Rarely. After being around here all day, I need time to myself." He'd given the explanation before he caught himself.

He quickly changed the subject. "Have you lured Theadora out of her cabin yet?" He hadn't meant to make it sound like a challenge, but that was the way it came out.

"This isn't a game, Mr. Crawford."

"I know that."

"Are you hoping I succeed with Theadora or fail?"

"I guess it has to be that cut-and-dry, doesn't it? No halfway. I thought she would just get rid of the veil with my dad...."

Abigail's expression softened at the obvious caring in his voice, a caring he was careful not to let get out of hand. "That would be a start. I expect success, but not instantly. And I won't be pushed into some kind of a dare so you can see me prove myself."

The woman was perceptive. He thought she'd be in a hurry to "fix" Theadora so she could boost her reputation and hook her career onto a star. But she seemed to be in no hurry. Could he be misjudging her? Why not? He'd misjudged his ex-wife. He'd thought bringing her here to this beautiful country could heal their hearts and their marriage. He'd been wrong.

Going to a side closet, he opened it, searched for a moment, then removed two poles. Standing one next to Abigail, he noted it would fit under her armpit. "That seems to be the right size. Do you have wool socks?'' Standing this close to her, he could faintly smell perfume, spicy flowers, something unusual, exotic. Or maybe her own woman's scent made it so.

Her eyes locked to his, she nodded. ''Anything else I need?''

Her voice sounded slightly breathless, and he wondered if the speed of her pulse matched his. But her throat was hidden by the slate-blue turtleneck she wore and the flower-patterned slate-and-mauve sweater over it was heavy and hid the beat of her heart. He couldn't keep his gaze from traveling over her blue corduroy slacks and her black boots. Imagining the curves under the clothes, he asked her gruffly, ''Are you really prepared for cross-country? If you don't do it often...''

''I'm in shape, if that's what you mean. I bicycle and jog, so my legs shouldn't give out.''

He remembered her legs encased in silk, her feet bare. Damn, he had to get a grip. If she didn't find anyone to ski with her, his father could take her. ''Good. Have fun skiing tomorrow. Snow's moving in again from what I hear, so you'll probably want to get an early start before it does.'' Stepping away from her, he closed the closet door. When he turned around, she murmured her thanks and added the poles to the skis over her shoulder. Taking the boots in her other hand, she slipped out of the room.

It was crazy, but he almost wished he had an excuse to talk to her longer. But he didn't. And from this moment on, he would make sure he was too busy to think about Ms. Abigail Fox, let alone talk to her.

Abigail dropped the ski equipment in her cabin, trying to forget the piercing intensity of Brady's green gaze, the shadows there that sometimes blackened to storm clouds. Not to mention the heat that seemed to sizzle between them when he stood close. Not even with Stan had she felt chemistry like that. But what good was chemistry without true love? Before Stan, she had believed that love could conquer all.

Abigail had developed a theory about men and women. Men wanted attractive women. The less attractive the man was, the less attractive the woman he chose. Unless, of course, he was powerful or rich. Those men felt they deserved models, too. And women... Women wished men would look beneath the surface right from the start. It took a special man to see underneath scars, to look beneath outside beauty.

Three years ago, Abigail had thought she'd found a special man who could. But she'd been wrong. He hadn't wanted "damaged" goods. Stan had said she'd gone out with him under false pretenses. If she'd told him sooner, would she be married to him now? Abigail still didn't know if the relationship had failed because of her nondisclosure or because of the stain on her face. So she advised her clients to always be upfront about their scars and whatever had happened to them.

Shaking her head, Abigail closed her cabin door and headed for Theadora's cabin. It was difficult to develop defenses and yet be open at the same time. She rapped on the door and waited. Yesterday, she'd dropped in on Theadora and they'd talked for over an hour. The actress loved recounting her "glory" years. Abigail had enjoyed it, too. It had given her a chance to know Theadora better and simply observe.

Theadora answered the door. It only took Abigail a moment to realize the actress was agitated—the stiff set of her slim body and the flutter of her hands were clear indicators. When she opened the door the whole way, Abigail saw why. Ethan Crawford stood in the small living room, his scowl broadcasting the tense atmosphere.

"If I'm interrupting, I can come back later."

Ethan motioned her inside. "Come in, Abigail. You're the one she needs to see. I don't know why in blazes she won't let you help her!"

Abigail understood the exasperation of significant others and family members. She'd dealt with scores of them. "Mr. Crawford, she has to be *ready* for my help."

He snapped his Stetson onto his head. "It's Ethan, Abigail. I already feel as old as Methuselah." He glanced significantly at Theadora. "Especially lately." Crossing to the door, he said, "I don't care what she looks like. We're friends. And I'm tired of never seeing her eyes. They're a beautiful hazel that change colors with her moods. I can't abide the fact she's hiding from me."

Abigail knew Theadora was hiding from herself, from the way she felt about herself, but she remained silent.

The actress turned away from them both and stubbornly sat on the sofa without saying a word.

Ethan swore. "I'll bring you supper at seven o'clock."

"That's not necessary," the actress said primly.

"The hell it's not. I guess you want to starve as well as wallow away. Well, I won't let you. I'll be here at seven, so be prepared for a rousing game of dominoes afterward." He closed the door with a loud thump.

Theadora dropped her hands into her lap and sighed.

"Do you believe him?" Abigail sat in the chair across from her.

"He probably cares less about my scars than I do. He always says what he means."

"He feels you're shutting him out."

"And I am. But what else can I do?"

"Let me evaluate you." Abigail saw the fear in the renewed stiffening of Theadora's body and knew the actress's answer. "You realize, don't you, that I've seen burn victims, accident victims, individuals with facial deformities? I'm a stranger, Theadora. I will look at you objectively and show you what I can do."

Theadora murmured, "That's why I brought you here. I hope you're not bored to death. I've given directions to the staff to give you anything you want or need."

"Theadora, let's get something straight. I'm here because I *want* to be here. But this is my vacation and I'm paying my own way. Except for my fee." She gave the older woman an encouraging smile. "Which you haven't let me earn yet."

The actress studied her and Abigail could feel an unasked question. Finally it came. "If I let you experiment with me, you will be the only person other than doctors and nurses who has seen my face since the accident. What will prevent you from selling my story, your reaction and anything else you want to put in it?"

Trust was the issue. Abigail didn't answer right away and finally decided, as always, that honesty was best. "Nothing will prevent me from doing that except my word. I won't exploit you, Theadora. That's not the way I've developed my career."

"I know. I've carefully looked into your background. But why do you do what you do? A pretty woman like you working with unhappy, broken-down people..."

"I want to help them find happiness again."

"In a makeup jar? Now you sound like the advertisers on Madison Avenue."

"Not in a makeup jar, but *inside*. The makeup gives my clients the strength to face life again."

Theadora studied Abigail pensively. "You didn't choose your profession on a whim. Why this?" she asked again.

"Because it gives me personal satisfaction."

Theadora tilted her head, and Abigail knew this lady might need more than verbal encouragement. She might have to see to believe. Abigail only used personal disclosure as a last resort. In this case, it might be necessary. When she was communing with nature tomorrow, she would have to give it serious thought.

Still not having found a skiing partner, Abigail left a note at the desk that evening saying she'd be ready to ski at 9:00 a.m. the next morning, conditions permitting. Snow could move in anytime, she supposed. Crested Butte was in one of the coldest areas of Colorado, and sometimes received record accumulations of snow.

The morning dawned with the hint of sun breaking through gray clouds. Abigail went to an early breakfast, sitting with a woman she'd met the day before, a customer-service representative from Boston who was also on a getaway vacation. Returning to her cabin,

Abigail stretched in preparation for her outing and dressed, expecting to see Ethan at her door when she heard the knock.

Her heart leapt when she saw Brady instead, standing there in black ski pants and jacket trimmed in red. He looked big and sleek and powerful, and she suddenly wanted to cancel her outing so she didn't have to deal with being alone with him.

"Are you ready?"

She gazed at the canteen slung over his head and under one arm instead of meeting his gaze. "I ... uh, didn't know whether to expect you or your dad."

"He went into town for decorations for the tree. We dropped a box and most of them broke. Said he had another errand, too. I don't ask questions."

"Does he?"

"No," Brady drawled. "We respect each other's privacy."

Abigail turned back into the room. She always put her foot in it with him. It had taken her many years to learn to speak her mind to someone other than her brother, to get over the idea that she was a bother and nothing she had to say was important. She'd lived in a corner too much of her life not for it to have an effect. Every day she reminded herself she was important and valuable, whether her stain was masked or not. Shrugging into her parka, she zipped it over her sweater and turtleneck.

Brady produced something from his pocket. "Here's a pair of gaiters. If you tie them around your ankles, they'll keep loose powder from melting inside your boots."

She extended her hand to take them. "Thank you. I don't own regular ski gear. I never had the time or opportunity to invest in it. I guess living here, you ski."

"I manage about once a week, twice if I'm lucky. It's good for the reflexes."

"You said you used to be a stuntman."

Brady let silence stand between them for a moment. "That's what I said."

She was being nosy, but didn't care. He intrigued her. "You've quit for good?"

"I stopped taking stunt jobs."

"An injury?"

"Something like that."

Brady's tight-lipped responses led her to ask, "Mind if I ask what drew you to stunt work?"

"My dad chauffeured scores of actors so I got to be around movie sets. The stunts fascinated me, and I learned firsthand how exacting a profession it was."

The faces of accident victims she'd seen and treated flashed before her eyes. "I don't understand how you can put yourself in danger like that, taking the chance of getting hurt. Not just the fights, but the car crashes—"

"It's all scientifically calculated. For a car crash, there would be a race car seat harness, I would wear a helmet. They would install a roll bar so the roof didn't collapse. The windshield is taken out and everything is padded."

"What about explosions? They use real cars, right?"

"We use miniature gas tanks to reduce the danger of fire."

"That's crazy!" she breathed.

His eyes narrowed. "Are you saying I'm crazy for choosing something I was good at, a career that was exciting and took me places I never would have gotten otherwise?"

She had no right to pass judgment on anyone. Her feelings were the result of seeing people forever maimed or disfigured in accidents they *couldn't* prevent. She just couldn't understand anyone inviting them. "Your career is your business, Mr. Crawford. Not mine. I'm sorry if I made it sound as if—"

"As if you don't approve?" He made a wry grimace. "You wouldn't be the first." He crouched down on the floor and held out a gaiter. "Step into this."

"What are you doing?"

"We'll get them on quicker this way."

"If you'd rather not ski with me, I can go alone."

"No one goes alone. Especially when they don't know the terrain or the trail. Come here."

His gaze ensnared hers, and male power exuded from him along with a heady masculine essence that spun her senses. Involuntarily, she took a few steps closer to him. His large hand nudged the heel of her boot. Lifting her foot, she aimed it for the gaiter and almost lost her equilibrium. She had to put her hand on Brady's shoulder for balance and felt as if she'd lost it again when she felt the hardness of his shoulder beneath his jacket. This was one sturdily built man.

Brady attached both gaiters and stood. "Let's go."

Abigail supposed *go* was a relative term. She was "going," but it was nothing like Brady's "going." Three or four times on cross country skis did not an expert make. And after remembering how to turn around, how to get both skis sliding in the same direction, she lagged behind Brady after the first thirty feet.

"How do you maintain the track?" Thank goodness they had one or she'd be even slower.

"Snowmobile attachment."

Brady's diagonal stride was smooth and swift.

Abigail paused for a moment and lifted her pole, adjusting the cotton headband on her wool cap. She was sweating already, but her makeup would be fine so long as she didn't rub her face.

Brady's weight shifted over his skis. He looked straight ahead and pressed his upper body forward. Abigail tried to keep to his rhythm, planting her poles for the best push. As the terrain angled uphill, she shortened her strides and her poling.

Brady stopped, his white puff of breath preceding his words. "Do you know how to ski uphill?"

Breaths seemed harder to come by. "Sidestepping?"

He nodded. "Or you can do the herringbone." He put his poles behind his skis and shifted the tails of his skis together to form a V. "You grip the hill with the inside edge."

Sidestepping seemed to take forever. She tried his way. More exertion, but faster climbing.

When they reached the top, she was breathless and lightheaded, but the view made her forget the physical sensations: forests of pine christened with white frosting; sparkles of hesitant sunlight reflecting from the smoother downhill track; mountaintops in the distance that even under a vibrant blue sky couldn't be more spectacular. The beauty wrapped around her, flowed through her, gave her chills, and she turned up her lips in a wide smile.

She felt Brady beside her before he said, "I've never seen country like this anywhere else."

"It makes me catch my breath. If I lived here, this would be one of my favorite spots."

"There are lots of them. Toward the back circle of the trail, there's a hollow not far from my house. No words can describe it."

"And that's what you named the lodge."

"I can't take the credit. The previous owners did that."

"Why did they sell?"

"Crested Butte has drawn more and more tourists each year with their free lift program at the start of the season, their expert ski trails that other resorts are afraid to have because of liability. The couple who owned Pine Hollow were getting older. They didn't want to be busier but did want to spend more time with their grandchildren in Denver. So they sold out and moved there."

"It would be hard to leave this."

"Yes, it would."

With Brady's beard and sunglasses she couldn't read his expression. "Did you keep the lodge the same?"

"We built the cabins, carved out this trail and I built my house. Basically, we wanted to keep the relaxed, getaway feeling that was here originally, because tourists come for that in the summer months, too."

"You've done that."

He shot her a quick glance. "Too isolated for you?"

"Oh, no. Not for a vacation."

"But you wouldn't like it all year."

"I don't know. I like people around me."

"Why?"

She could hide from him, give him a clichéd answer. *Avoid danger,* an inner voice whispered. But the view, the hushed silence and Brady beside her, urged her to give a truthful answer to a not-idly asked question. "I spent many years keeping to myself. Once I learned to enjoy people, I found it added dimension to my life that wasn't there before." Holding her breath, she waited for the questions, questions she didn't know if she would dodge or answer. She wished she could see his eyes.

A moment later, she didn't have to worry about answering anything. He shifted on his skis and motioned to the downhill track before them. "Will you be able to handle the slope?"

The slope? Sure. She'd just averted much more hazardous terrain. "I'll be fine."

Abigail managed to snowplow down the hill. She held the tips of her skis together and fanned out the tails. It prevented her from going too fast. Brady skied downhill with one ski ahead of the other, his front leg dropped in a deep bend at the knee. His movements were slick, expert. He waited for her at the bottom.

They'd been skiing more level ground with the track curving between snow-frosted evergreens when she began to feel nauseated. Her heart throbbed between her ears and the vague dizziness she'd experienced earlier became more persistent. But she couldn't stop. She didn't want to look like a wimp.

Another fifteen minutes and they faced another hill. Abigail decided to use the sidestep but couldn't make her skis go where she wanted them. Gulping in breaths that didn't seem to be big enough, she tried putting the back of her skis together as Brady had shown her. She'd managed three Vs and had poked her poles into the snow behind her when the dizziness and nausea hit in a wave at the same time.

She couldn't think as she began to topple but she managed, "Brady!" before the grayness swirled around her and she closed her eyes to shut it out.

Chapter Three

Brady heard his name and knew Abigail was in trouble before he turned around. She'd slowed down, and he should have checked on her. But every time he talked to her and got drawn into her questions, her probing blue eyes, he felt as if he stood on the edge of a cliff.

As he turned he saw her hit the snow, and his heart almost stopped. Skiing to her, he called her name. She didn't answer. Quickly flipping off his skis, he knelt beside her. "Abigail. Abigail! Come on, open your eyes." He took off her sunglasses and laid them beside her head.

Feeling the pulse at her neck, he noted it was fast but strong. Suddenly she stirred. Her tongue dipped out to lick her lips, and her eyes fluttered open. "Brady?"

His given name sounded much too right on those lips. Crisis knocked down barriers because he'd used hers, too. Naturally, without thinking. Well, he'd better think now. And clearly. He knew he shouldn't lift her or move her until he knew what had happened. "Tell me what's wrong. Did you lose your footing?"

"No. I've been feeling a little dizzy...."

"And you didn't tell me?"

"I thought it would go away," she murmured.

"Anything else?"

"Nausea right before I...I passed out. But I'm sure I'm okay now." She tried to sit up. "It must have been the cold, the exercise..."

"Stay still for a minute," he commanded. "Does anything hurt?"

She moved her arms and legs. "No. I feel so stupid. I'm sure I'm all right."

He put his arms under her shoulders to raise her upper body. Even through the layers of clothing she felt delicate, fragile. Her blue gaze drifted over his expression. He couldn't have felt more sensation if she'd touched him. Pushing down the sudden surge of desire, he said gruffly, "You're not all right. You have altitude sickness."

"I don't understand." The quick flutter of her long auburn lashes told him she was still woozy and fighting it.

"I thought you'd had enough time to get used to it. Because you were in shape, I didn't think it would be a problem. But too much exertion too soon can bring it on."

"The skiing did this?"

Taking off his glove, he reached inside her collar. She started. Her warm, smooth skin scorched his finger; her turtleneck was damp with perspiration. "This air is thinner and drier. You need to get used to that. Exertion dehydrates you. You need to drink plenty of liquids but stay away from alcohol and caffeine."

"I had a half a cup of coffee before we left."

He grimaced and shook his head. "Let's see how you're doing." When he helped her into a sitting position, her lids fluttered shut again. "Open your eyes and take deep, slow breaths. It'll help."

She did as he suggested and gave him an apologetic smile.

Remorse swamped him. She had nothing to apologize for; this was his fault. He should have told her to wait to ski; he should have realized what was happening sooner. If he'd taken a few minutes back there when they'd stopped to really talk to her... Hell, all he'd been interested in was getting this jaunt over with and keeping his distance. Because of him, she'd probably feel miserable for the rest of the day.

His arm still around her, the desire to pull her close and kiss her was stronger and more penetrating than the cold surrounding him. When he leaned toward her, she tilted up her chin, a multitude of questions in her eyes—questions that could lead him to dig up the past. His ex-wife. Her miscarriage. Cole's accident.

No! Abigail Fox would be here a few weeks, then she'd leave. He wasn't stupid enough to bring pain to the surface for no good reason.

Dropping his arm, he waited to see if she was steady before he leaned away. She took a few more deep breaths. Reaching for his canteen, he lifted it over his head, uncapped it and offered it to her. "Take a few mouthfuls to get some liquid into you. But slowly."

Abigail took it from him, holding it with two hands. He watched her lips surround the opening, lips that were darkened slightly by a rosy lipstick, as natural as the rest of her flawlessly applied makeup. He'd been around enough women, particularly actresses, to know when a woman wore makeup and when she didn't. Though it seemed silly to him that Abigail would wear it skiing, he also knew many women were either vain enough, or insecure enough, not to step outside their house without it. Except...Abigail didn't seem either vain or insecure.

Hell, what did he know about her? Not enough to draw any conclusions.

As Abigail swallowed the water slowly and a drop of the liquid stood on her lower lip, Brady's body tightened, his pulse thudding where he could feel it most. All he could think about again was kissing her, tasting her, remembering what passion could be.

"Let's try standing." His voice sounded as rough as the splintered chips in his wood box.

"Should I take off my skis?"

Her fall had been gentle so her skis had stayed attached to her boots. "Let's see how you do with them on. You'll sink in too deep with just your boots. But before we try it, drink a little more."

She did, breathing slowly in between swallows. Then she handed the canteen back to him. After capping it, he hung it over his shoulder. Putting his arm around her waist, he lifted her to her feet. He could feel her sway, then right herself.

"This would be easier on level ground," she said with a small smile.

Wanting to support her, but being tempted by standing so close, he asked, "Think you can stand by yourself?"

She nodded, and he stooped to retrieve her sunglasses and poles. He kept a close eye on her as he handed her her sunglasses. She seemed to be steady. "Keep taking slow, deep breaths."

"Do we have far to go?"

He reattached his skis to his boots. "There's a shortcut, an alternate trail we use for begin—if we want to get back quickly. Once we're down this hill, it'll be easygoing."

Her gaze locked to his. It was as if he were grounding her.

When they began the trip back, Abigail sidestepped gingerly, still breathing deeply, trying to keep her knees from wobbling, trying not to feel like a complete fool. She'd never fainted in her life! And to do it in front of Brady...

He was watching her closely, and she knew he wasn't going to take his eyes off her. That added to her shaky knees.

"We're going to do this real slow and keep exertion to a minimum. I'd let you rest longer, but it's too cold to stay still long."

Abigail couldn't agree more. Her clothes felt damp underneath, and chills crawled up her back.

At the top of the hill, she stopped for a moment and dug her poles into the snow. Brady was beside her before she could blink. His jacket sleeve rustled against hers before he supported her by cupping her elbow. "How do you feel? And tell me the truth."

"Worried you'll have to carry me?" she managed to tease as she fought the unsteadiness. At least the nausea hadn't returned.

"Worried? Nah. Concerned, maybe."

She smiled. "You could leave me here and go get a sled."

"I wouldn't leave you here alone," he returned gruffly.

She'd been trying to lighten the situation but he wouldn't let her. Such a serious man. Touching his arm, she said, "I'm all right. A little lightheaded. I'll yell if I feel worse."

Brady nodded and looked down at her hand on his arm. She took it away. He stayed beside her as they snowplowed down the hill. When they came to a fork, he guided her to the left. The trail led past Brady's log home. She wanted to take a better look, but she was so tired, she could hardly put one ski in front of the other.

When she glided to a stop at her cabin door, she shook. Taking her key from her pocket, she dropped it in the snow. Brady unfastened the bindings on his skis and plucked the wooden ring from the depression it had made when it had fallen. But before he opened her door, he unhooked her bindings. She didn't bother to protest but saved her energy for stepping from them and leaning her poles against the cabin.

Brady opened her door and they went inside. She headed toward the sofa, but Brady's smoky voice stopped her. "You go change while I get you something to drink."

Her arms felt too heavy to lift, her legs like sticks that weren't connected to her. She took one look at the bed and knew if she sat on it, she wouldn't get up again for a very long time. Peeling off the layers of clothing sapped another level of strength. She felt chilled, so instead of the satin robe she'd brought along, she pulled on the royal blue sweat suit she wore in the evenings.

When she returned to the living room, Brady was waiting with a glass of mineral water. "It's better if you drink it without ice. I'll bring you some juices so you can keep drinking. Stay away from the hot chocolate. All the teas are herbal so they're okay. Would you like me to make you a cup?"

She took the glass from him and sank down on the sofa. He'd removed his hat, jacket and sunglasses. His ski pants' bib top came up over his gray cableknit sweater. His hair was disheveled from his cap. "You have better things to do than to nursemaid me. The way I feel now, I'll probably fall asleep for the rest of the day."

"Your adrenaline has stopped pumping. You're going to have to take it easy for a while and let your body recover and adjust."

He looked so concerned, so guilty. "This wasn't your fault, Brady."

His dark eyebrows raised and his jaw stiffened. "Yes, it was. I should have asked questions. I should have been watching you more closely. That was a dangerous situation out there. You could sue me for negligence."

He was overreacting, and all she wanted to do was bring a smile to his face. "Sue you for negligence? When we've just gotten to a first-name basis? I don't think so."

No amusement flickered in his eyes. No relief. He was taking full responsibility and that was that. She sighed. "I'll make a cup of tea later."

He took a few steps closer. "What would you like for lunch? I'll have it sent to your cabin."

She didn't like anyone making decisions for her. "I'm not hungry. Besides, what if I feel like going out?"

"Abigail, trust me. It's better if you curl up with a good book."

"Are you this overprotective with all your guests?"

"My guests don't usually faint on the trail."

"I'm not going to be able to live this down," she grumbled.

He almost smiled. Almost. Towering above her, he reached out and smoothed his hand across her left temple.

She reared back. "What's wrong?"

"A mark from your cap."

She felt for herself. Usually she didn't worry about her makeup. But with Brady examining her so closely she wished she'd checked it. There was a ridge from the cotton band. Experience told her it should be fine but with everything that had happened . . .

It wasn't everything that had happened. She could trust the makeup. She couldn't trust Brady's response if he saw her defect.

"Your hair reminds me of a brand-new penny when the sun hits it."

Pushing away her insecurity, she smiled. "I guess that's why my brother describes me as strawberry-blond sometimes and auburn others."

"Is he older or younger?"

"Kent's older."

"You're fond of him."

"Very."

"Any other brothers or sisters?"

"An older sister. How about you?"

"None."

Brady's expression was inscrutable, or maybe his beard just made it seem to be. However, when she gazed into his eyes, she saw loneliness—deep and hurtful. She'd known loneliness and connected with it in many of her clients. But she was sure Brady wouldn't tell her about his.

It didn't take a fast learner to discover he was a man of few personal words. Theadora had said Brady had experienced hard times, too. Was that the reason? "How long have you and your dad lived here?"

"Nine years."

"So it really feels like home."

"I suppose. Home's a state of mind rather than a place."

She tilted her head and thought about it. "Maybe so."

"Drink," he encouraged, nodding to the glass in her hand.

She took a few swallows, then set the glass on the table. Brady was still watching her as if afraid she'd disintegrate before his eyes. Commandeering every last iota of energy to show him she was made of sterner stuff than that, she stood and faced him nose-to-nose. Well, stockinged feet to boots, anyway. "I'm going to take a nap, Brady. Unless you want to watch me sleep, you might as well leave."

He didn't back away but lifted her chin with his knuckle to scrutinize her thoroughly. "I'm concerned because you don't have a phone. And if you feel dizzy again..."

The rough texture of his skin created a tingling that spread down her neck through the rest of her body. "I promise I won't move from the bed until dinner. Will that satisfy you?"

"I could send one of the staff to stay with you."

The longing his touch created, besides his stubbornness, made her say sharply, "That's *not* necessary."

Answering sparks of determination lit his eyes. "I have a master key. I'll be back to check on you in an hour."

When Abigail traveled, she never forgot to double-lock her door. Even this cabin had a chain lock she'd fastened both nights. But for some irrational reason, she trusted this man she barely knew. "All right." The concession and her physical reaction to Brady depleted what was left of her energy.

Brady must have seen that. He held her by the shoulders and gazed deeply into her eyes. "Rest. I'll be back."

He was so close. She could feel his breath across her cheek. If he bent his head...

But he didn't. He let go of her and backed away. She managed to stay on her feet until he zippered his jacket, pulled on his hat and closed the door behind him. Then she collapsed on the sofa, laid her head against the arm, closed her eyes and gave in to the tide of fatigue.

The dead bolt turned almost silently. If Abigail was sleeping, Brady didn't want to wake her. He shifted the bag in his arms when he saw her lying on the sofa. For a moment, he just stared. She couldn't be comfortable. Her hands lay under her cheek on the sofa arm. She was curled into a ball as if she were cold.

He stowed a quart of orange juice and a bottle of grape juice in her refrigerator, then went to her bedroom. Jars of makeup were scattered across her small dresser. A sketch pad sat on the corner. Did she draw? Paint?

Lifting a pillow from the bed, he carried it to the closet, where he pulled an extra blanket from the top shelf. He took them to the living room. She looked so feminine with her hair caressing her cheek, her pink-tipped nails peeking out from under her chin. He would carry her to her bed, but he was afraid she'd wake up and object. Or maybe he was just afraid she'd wake up, and he'd want to do more than carry her to the bed.

Gently he lifted her head and attempted to tuck the pillow underneath. She stirred, and when she did, he managed to wedge it under her shoulders. Knowing comfort even while asleep, she nestled into the pillow, securing it in an ideal position. Brady almost smiled as she snuggled again like a kitten settling in for a long nap.

Unfolding the blanket, he pulled it up over her shoulders. She seemed to relax under its warmth as she stretched her legs out instead of curling them to her stomach. He knew he should leave. But he told himself he was just making sure the rise and fall of her breathing was regular. It was.

He didn't know how long he stood there. But he did know if he didn't get moving, he'd start asking questions. Like—was she as sweet as she seemed? Was she here for more than monetary reasons? Did she really care about what happened to Theadora?

He didn't want to ask the questions, and he certainly didn't want to search for the answers. Because in the process he might feel something again. And that would hurt.

So he ignored the questions and, after a last long look, left Abigail Fox to her nap.

Until six-thirty, when he arrived at her door, dinner in hand, and the cabin was still dark. She'd missed lunch; he didn't want her to miss dinner. As he opened the door, he didn't try to be quiet. It was time for Sleeping Beauty to wake up. Flipping on the light, he set the disposable containers of food on the table and fished appropriate silverware out of the drawer. He was aware of her the instant she moved.

Abigail blinked and sat up, holding the blanket up to her chin, trying to orient herself. Then in a husky voice that sent blood rushing to male parts he'd consigned to functional use, she said, "Brady?"

"Time for dinner." He turned toward the cupboard and removed a soup bowl and bread plate.

Abigail slid her fingers along the satin edge of the blanket and dug her elbow into the pillow. "I guess you provided these?"

He shrugged. "From the bedroom." He remembered the softness of her hair as he'd placed the pillow under her head.

Running her fingers through her hair, she yawned and flipped her legs over the side of the sofa. Her nose twitched as he opened the containers of food. "I'll be right back," she mumbled as she picked up the blanket and pillow and disappeared into the bedroom.

She'd looked steady on her feet, but it had been hard for Brady to tell.

She returned a few minutes later, her hair combed into place. Sitting at the table, she gave him a tentative smile. "You didn't have to do this."

"I thought you should keep it light. Chicken noodle soup, French bread, baked apples. Are you hungry?"

"Now that I smell it, I am. Have you eaten?"

"Yep. There's more juice in the refrigerator. The more liquids, the better you'll feel. How's the dizziness?"

Opening the pat of butter, she spread it on the bread. "It's almost gone." She ran her gaze over his jacket. "You could stay and keep me company."

He should get going—and fast. "Theadora called and asked if I'd seen you. I told her what happened."

"Shoot. I was supposed to stop in this afternoon. I'll go over tomorrow. I hope you told her I'm fine."

"I told her I'd be checking on you again." He moved toward the door.

Abigail laid down the spoon, pushed her chair back and followed him. At the door, she said, "Thank you. I still feel so foolish...."

"Abigail, this happens. I've seen six-foot hulking skiers used to Connecticut or Northern California who think they can fly in here one day, ski the next, but end up flat on their backs. Don't overdo it the next couple of days, and you'll be fine."

She was the picture of innocence, sweetness, caring. Could he believe those qualities lived inside the woman? Carol had been sweet, too. But she hadn't been able to accept his work, and his work had cost them their child. Neither of them had been able to get beyond that.

He could indulge in an affair if Abigail was willing. Maybe that was exactly what he needed to calm the restlessness that had been unsettling him lately. She was close enough to touch, almost close enough to taste. All he had to do was reach out....

Then she smiled. An open, vulnerable smile that slugged him right in the gut. He opened the door. Snow fell, layering the area with pure white powder.

"Oh, isn't it gorgeous!"

"The snow's what I like best about this area."

"Build many snowmen?"

"We can't. The snow's too dry at this altitude."

"How about snow angels?" she teased.

He smiled. "I've never tried." He'd like nothing better than to make snow angels with Abigail. His smile faded as he pulled his cap out of his pocket and stretched it onto his head. "Enjoy dinner."

"Thank you. For everything."

He stepped into winter, away from her warmth and her voice. With a wave of his hand, he hiked toward his house, suddenly wishing it felt more like a home.

The dining room bustled with guests who were headed for or had just finished sampling the array of breakfast foods from the buffet line. Abigail's apple pancakes teased her with their sweet cinnamon aroma. Seeing a few people she'd eaten with previously, she walked toward their table.

But a tap on the shoulder and a familiar presence stopped her. Last night, she'd felt she and Brady had connected in some way—as people did when they'd shared an experience or found common ground. The flash of desire in his eyes right before he'd left had made a part of her wish the little guardian angel inside her head was not shaking a you-should-know-better finger at her.

This morning Brady looked anything but friendly. His sheepskin jacket hung open, his gloves peeked out of his pocket. He held his sunglasses in one hand as he frowned and said briskly, "I have a message for you."

"From Theadora?"

"No. From Video Concepts. They'd like to talk to you about your script." He dug into his pocket and produced a small slip of white paper. "Here's the number."

"I have it back at the cabin."

"I'll bet you do."

"Excuse me?"

"Never mind." He looked her up and down. "It seems as if you've recovered."

She pointed to the two small glasses of juice and smiled, hoping he'd smile back. "No dizziness and still drinking."

Brady nodded, a brisk, final nod as if his job as caretaker was over. "Good. Now you can get on with your...vacation. Have a good day."

She watched him weave through the tables to the door. Have a good day? What had happened between last night and this morning to bring back that cold politeness?

Brady was splitting the last log for the day when Luke appeared in his backyard. "Early, aren't you?"

"Got out early."

Brady bet ten to one Luke had cut his last class or two. The boy was headed for trouble, but all Brady could do was listen. Luke was rarely in a "taking advice" mode unless it came to stunts.

Brady brought the ax down into the splitting stump. That was enough for today. Sometimes his ten-plus years in the stunt business took a toll on his forty-year-old body.

Luke came up to the logs scattered alongside the stump. "Need help carrying this inside, or does it go to the cabins?"

"Inside."

Brady stacked the wood in his arms as Luke did the same. The teenager stared straight ahead as he walked down the snow-covered path. "Dad and Sheila are gettin' married in March."

Will Underwood owned the ranch that butted up against Pine Hollow's property. Brady respected Luke's father and had spent many a Friday evening with Will as he'd tried to get over the loss of his wife. "Sheila's good for your dad, Luke. He's been lonely since your mom died."

Luke kept his gaze averted. "I guess so."

"Are you helping to plan the wedding?"

The teenager grimaced. "I'd rather scope babes."

Brady bit back a wry smile as he recognized Luke's change of subject. "Tourists are pouring in again."

"Sure are. But your Miss Fox beats anything *I've* seen."

"She's not my Miss Fox."

Luke shot him a speculative look. "How long's she staying?"

"She's booked for a month, but I don't know if she'll stay that long."

"You interested?"

Brady's relationship with Luke had evolved over the years into a big brotherlike friendship. "Attracted but not interested."

"Why?"

Good question. Probably because she'd already gotten under his skin without half trying. Unless she was an awfully good actress. With what he'd found out about her today, that was likely. Making a video. She wanted to get into the big time, all right.

He answered Luke with the simplest explanation he could find. "She's not my type."

Besides the message Brady had given her that morning, Abigail had a stack of calls she should make—speaking engagements she needed to confirm, doctors to call who had patients to refer in the next few months. She wanted to call Kent and find out how he was spending Christmas. But she didn't have access to a phone. She'd tried to find Ethan, but no one knew where he was. Apparently he and Brady took turns being on-call for emergencies, and it was Brady's night.

That left her no recourse but to search him out. After asking several employees, a waiter setting up the dining room for dinner told her that Brady had said he'd be at his house for the evening doing bookkeeping. So she hiked to his front porch, not knowing what type of welcome she'd receive.

The house had a rough-hewn quality, like Brady, but also distinctive features that showed he'd probably played a part in its design. It was L-shaped, the double-car garage lengthening the L that was constructed of logs. The short part of the L consisted of multicolor stone. An octagonal window sat in the roof's point. The porch was small, outlined with cedar railing. No wreath hung on Brady's door. That seemed unusual when the lodge and the cabins abounded with evergreen boughs and arrangements.

Lifting the brass knocker, she let it fall. The sound didn't carry so she did it again, ducking her chin into her collar as the wind blew. When Brady still didn't appear, she banged the knocker as hard as she could twice more. Maybe the waiter had been wrong or Brady had changed his mind.

The wind whistled through the trees as it picked up velocity, and a few snow flurries flittered against the darkening sky. After dinner she was going to curl up in front of her fireplace and make some changes on the script before she called Video Concepts tomorrow. She'd spent the morning going through it one last time. The afternoon she'd spent talking with Theadora, becoming more sure she'd have to show the actress firsthand what she could do for her.

Ready to turn away and search for Ethan after dinner, Abigail rapped one last time.

The door opened and her jaw dropped in surprise. Brady stood there, bare feet, bare legs, bare everything except a mammoth white towel wrapped around his hips, looking at her as if she were the last person on earth he'd imagine at his door. His shoulders were broad, still showing evidence of a summer tan, and ridged with muscle that defined his upper arms. Whorls of black hair swirled across his chest. A waving line still dewed with drops of water disappeared under his towel. Male force, pulsating power, emanated from him, and Abigail was much too aware that he was a man and she was a woman.

Clearing her throat, she dredged up her voice. "I guess this is a bad time."

His black brows arched. "That depends."

"On?"

"Whether or not you like hot tubs. Care to join me?"

Chapter Four

Brady had no idea why that question had popped out. Maybe because the fantasy dogged his dreams. Maybe because he wanted to see her reaction. Maybe because she made him feel as if he were thawing after being frozen for years.

"Uh ... I didn't bring my bathing suit this trip. No hot tubs for me," Abigail answered, sounding a bit breathless.

He didn't suggest the alternative to wearing a bathing suit, but she must have followed the drift of his thoughts because she avoided his gaze and took a step back. "I ... uh, need to use a phone."

Moving to the side, he said, "You can use mine."

"No. Not right now. I mean ..."

"Abigail, why don't you come in? I'm not dressed for the windchill."

Her eyes traveled again over his bare chest, making him feel anything but cold. The rush of blood to his groin made him angry with her, angry with himself.

She scurried inside, mumbling, "Sorry."

As she stood on the braided rug, snow slipping from her boots, he said, "I'll give you privacy if you need it." When she looked at him, perplexed, he added, "To make the phone call."

She jammed her gloved hands into her pockets as if she didn't know what to do with them. "It's not just one call. That's the problem. I have a slew of business calls to make. Is there someplace I can go tomorrow morning, an empty room or..."

"You can use the office in the lodge behind the reception desk," he answered gruffly.

"Will anyone need to use the office?"

"Are you going to be on the phone all morning?"

"No. Probably an hour—"

"Then don't worry about it."

"But, Brady..."

"It's not your fault the cabin doesn't have a phone. We'll survive the inconvenience."

"I chose the cabin," she said softly.

His hand went to the place where his towel was tucked in at his waist. "Abigail, it's no big deal."

"I might have to do this more than once. Are you sure you don't mind me using the phone now and then?"

Frustrated by feelings he didn't understand, he shot back, "Why should I mind? We have a lot of guests who have to deal with business while they're here. Lord knows, I wouldn't want to stand between you and a deal with Video Concepts."

She look puzzled. "What's wrong, Brady?"

"Nothing's wrong."

"You could have fooled me. Yesterday you became almost friendly, today we're back to polite. Did I do something? Say something?"

He'd never expected her to be so honest. "No, it's not what you said or did. It's your motives that bother me."

"What motives? I'm here to help Theadora."

"Why? Because she'll help you get where you want to go?"

"And where do I want to go?" she asked, sounding confused.

"Probably to Hollywood. Do makeup for people who matter. Maybe get into the movie industry. You wouldn't be the first. Each client is a stepping-stone."

She gave him a penetrating stare. "Is this leftover thinking from your stint in Hollywood?"

"Leftover? I don't think so. Everyone has an angle. Nothing's for free. I scratch your back, you scratch mine. It's what makes the world go 'round."

Her expression softened. "I thought love did that."

Old pain stabbed him so hard, his voice lowered a register. "Love's overrated."

She tilted her head and her auburn waves slid against her cheek. "I see. And a cynical viewpoint isn't?"

Feeling uncomfortable, he shifted his stance, his hand tightening on the towel as he thought about flipping off her hat and running his fingers through her hair. "Cynical has nothing to do with it. I've seen how people use each other."

"So have I. I try not to use anybody, Brady. I don't know what you think I do, but taking Theadora as a client is unusual for me. I work with ordinary people, usually in hospitals, people whose lives were changed by accidents, by fires, by fate."

"Then where does Video Concepts fit in? You're not going to sell your skill, your products?"

"I'm doing the video for a foundation for burn victims. It will teach doctors, nurses, survivors and students of cosmetology. Any profit will go to the foundation."

Although she spoke in an even cadence, her blue eyes flashed silver sparks, and he bet she was holding on to her temper. "If what you say is true..."

"That's the problem with becoming jaded, Brady. You can't tell the truth from a lie. That's a shame." She opened the door. When it closed behind her, the near slam was the only indication of the tight rein she'd held on her temper.

Brady watched her walk down the path to the cabins. She hadn't raised her voice, or argued, or taken potshots. She'd spoken the truth and made him feel like a first-class jerk.

The great room at the lodge buzzed with the voices of guests gathered to socialize around the roaring fire. But Brady was only interested in finding one particular guest. He found Abigail almost dead center in the grouping of chairs. She was smiling and speaking to the businessman from cabin four. The businessman with the suave smile, blond perfectly combed hair and impeccable manners. Brady had watched the man entertain more than one single woman guest at the lodge over the two years he'd been coming. And there Abigail was with him, laughing, talking...

Without thinking about it once, let alone twice, Brady approached them. "Abigail, could I have a few words with you?"

She stood and smiled at Jim Stover—with a little too much enthusiasm in Brady's estimation—as she said, "I'll be right back."

"You will sit with me at dinner?" Stover asked.

"Sure."

He stood, too. "Then why don't I find us a nice table?"

Abigail nodded and with a side glance at Brady, Stover left them.

Unsettled by the thought of them having dinner together, Brady asked, "Have you two been acquainted long?"

Abigail's eyes held a wariness not there previously. "No. We just started talking when I came over for dinner."

Silence stretched between them, and Brady knew he'd have to break it. Guests milled about within earshot so he motioned toward the French doors. "Let's go over there where it's quieter."

Abigail followed his lead without question or protest. At the edge of the room, she waited expectantly.

Feeling as if this was one of the more adventuresome stunts he'd executed over the years, Brady plunged in. "I'm sorry, Abigail. I had no right to judge you or your profession."

"No, you didn't," she agreed with a lift of her auburn brows.

"I've known Theadora a long time. She's been sheltered over the years by her agent, her business manager, even her housekeeper. She rarely deals with the world directly."

"She heard about my work from her doctor, Brady. Not a television commercial."

"Since her accident, she's been hounded by reporters who want to exploit her."

"That explains why she doesn't trust me yet. She's afraid I'll talk to the press, I guess, or at the worst a tabloid reporter."

After a thoughtful moment, he concluded, "You wouldn't do that."

"You weren't very sure of that an hour ago."

"I should have been. I should have listened to my intuition rather than my experience. Will you accept my apology?"

After studying him and his sincerity, she smiled and extended her hand. "Apology accepted."

He felt too relieved to explain the reaction to himself. His fingers wrapped around hers, and he found he didn't want to let go of her softness, of her warmth, of her caring. He also didn't want her spending too much time with Jim Stover. "Have you planned anything for tomorrow?"

She left her hand in his. "Nothing in particular. I'm spending the morning with Theadora after I make my calls."

He rubbed his thumb over the tender skin between her thumb and forefinger as he asked, "How would you like to come with me to cut down a Christmas tree for the lodge?"

She hesitated only a second. "I'd like that very much. If we don't have to ski," she teased.

"You're feeling all right?"

"I'm fine. I just thought I'd wait a couple of days before trying it again."

His lips twitched in an answering smile. "No skis. Snowmobile. All you have to do is hold on."

"That sounds easy enough."

He thought about her arms wrapped around him, her body pressed against his. "Less exertion than riding a motorcycle."

"What time?"

"About three?"

"Three's good."

Brady had a tough time unlocking his gaze from hers, let alone releasing her hand. But somehow he managed it. "I won't keep you from dinner any longer."

"You could join us."

He was tempted. He could sit between her and Stover. Impatiently, he dismissed the thought. "I have to spend the night at the computer." He took a step back so he didn't change his mind. "Dress warm tomorrow."

"I will."

Before he took her back to his cabin for dinner and dreamed about her sitting in his hot tub, he said, "I'll see you tomorrow, then."

She nodded, and he reluctantly walked away.

Although she'd warned herself against it, Abigail was excited about her afternoon with Brady. His apology had been sincere and for a moment, just a moment, it had sounded as if it mattered to him whether she accepted his invitation or not. But in case she was wrong, she was trying to keep her enthusiasm in check. She knew all too well how quickly disappointment could follow on its heels.

Pushing the afternoon to the back of her mind, she shifted her makeup carrier to her left hand and rapped on Theadora's cabin door. She'd phoned the actress from the lodge when she'd made her other calls. As always when she was about to disclose her secret, Abigail was nervous. But sweaty palms wouldn't get in the way of showing Theadora something she needed to see.

Theadora opened the door, her pale blue wool skirt and matching sweater setting off her delicate figure perfectly. Abigail smiled. "Are you having lunch with Ethan?"

"Around noon. I'm going to miss him terribly when I leave."

"I want you to give me the chance to help you before you do."

Theadora noticed the makeup case. "Oh, Abigail, the thought of taking off this veil, even for you..."

Abigail went to the table and set the makeup case on it. Opening it, she took out a mirror and stood it up. "I want to show you something." She took off her jacket and tossed it to the sofa. As she picked up the jar of makeup remover and a cotton pad, she sat down in front of the mirror. Applying the cream, she rubbed it in until the makeup liquified, then she wiped with the patch of cotton.

Theadora came to the other side of the table. "Abigail, I'm sure the products you use are fine quality, but—" She stopped abruptly and Abigail heard the small gasp as the port-wine stain on the left side of her face appeared. It ran from above her left brow to the line of her mouth under her cheekbone.

Abigail put more specially designed cleansing cream on the side of her face and wiped again. The purplish stain was large. And without cover, as she had as a child, she felt self-conscious. Overcoming the feeling for at least the millionth time, she lifted her face to Theadora.

"My dear, I never expected...I'm so sorry, I..."

"Theadora, relax. You can't possibly have a reaction I haven't seen or heard. It's a birthmark. And I've treated clients who have to deal with much worse."

"But you've had it..."

"All my life. Until I found the wonderful lady who created this makeup and she showed me how to cover it. I'd had some experience with greasepaint, but it didn't look natural. And when I found this and she showed me what to do, I knew I had to help others the same way. My life changed drastically after I looked 'normal' again. I don't know what that says for society, but I had fought so many years to be accepted, I welcomed this camouflage. I went to cosmetology school, started dating for the first time in my life. I could actually feel pretty."

"How does it look so natural? I couldn't even tell!"

"It's the way the makeup is created in bases and tints to match your complexion perfectly. Come sit beside me and I'll show you."

Theadora watched Abigail take the jars from her makeup case. "A plastic surgeon couldn't do anything about your birthmark?" She sat beside Abigail and lifted one of the jars to study the label.

"Surgery and chemical freezing can leave scars that are worse than the birthmark. Doctors now are experimenting with laser-beam therapy that can lighten the stain, but with this makeup, I can cover it and no one knows it's there." Theadora was staring at her. Abigail was used to it and didn't flinch.

"Regular makeup doesn't work?"

"No. The stain creeps through. Now watch and imagine me helping you." Abigail mixed a tiny amount of pink into her light beige basic shade to match her fair skin. The pink added life to the color.

Abigail pressed the makeup on her birthmark, feathering it and smoothing it. Then, she took a puff and patted it into the powder. "This is a sealing powder. It waterproofs the foundation and makes it feel like a second skin."

Theadora pushed her finger into the powder and examined it. "This waterproofs?"

"Did you read the book and information I sent you?"

The actress avoided facing her. "No. I've been so afraid to hope...."

"It waterproofs it," Abigail repeated, ignoring Theadora's embarrassment. "Now, it's not rub-proof. If I went swimming and rubbed my face, it would come off. But normally it lasts until you take it off." She nodded to the jar. "Go ahead and feel the makeup. See how it smooths on if you'd like."

"No, I don't think so...."

"On the back of your hand, Theadora. See how it blends."

Abigail took out another tint and encouraged the actress to experiment. By adding a yellow tint in differing amounts, she saw how the color became the exact shade of her skin.

Abigail took a soft brush and swept lightly over the layer of powder on her face. "All finished."

"It's absolutely amazing! I'd never know."

"That's the idea. I can go on with my life and no one takes a second look."

Theadora reached under her veil and Abigail realized she was touching her scars pensively. "You think you can do that for me?"

"I don't know. My blemish is smooth. If you have scars, you probably have some raised tissue."

"The plastic surgeon did what he could. The small ones are fairly smooth. But the one across my cheek is hideous. There's the possibility that if I have another surgery, it will make it worse rather than better. And there's always the possibility of nerve damage...."

"Are your scars worse than my face without makeup?"

"Oh, no, but—"

"Let me try."

Theadora again picked up a jar and turned it around in her hand. "I'll never make another movie. The camera sees too much."

"What about just living a normal life?"

"I haven't had a 'normal' life for as long as I can remember. People think stars live glamorous lives. We can buy anything we want, we have people at our beck and call, but life can be lonely. Especially since Ethan moved out here. Talking on the phone isn't the same."

"Are you and Ethan more than friends?"

"I've always wanted more. But Ethan has this male pride that always gets in the way."

"Wouldn't it be wonderful to see him face-to-face again without the veil?" Abigail knew it was a slightly manipulative question, but she felt the actress was teetering near the edge of decision.

"Yes, it would. And maybe..." She studied Abigail's face carefully. "Let me read the material you sent me."

Abigail smiled. "Fair enough. If you want me before I get back to you, if you have any questions, call the desk and leave a message for me. I'll check there when I get back."

"Where are you going?" Theadora asked wistfully.

"To cut down a Christmas tree."

"With Ethan and Brady?"

"With Brady."

Theadora studied Abigail's face again, then smiled enigmatically. "Maybe you can take some of his sadness away."

That statement raised more questions than Abigail could count. "We're only going to cut down a tree."

Theadora slowly shook her head. "Um. Brady doesn't ask just anyone to do something like that."

Theadora's words tumbled around in Abigail's head that afternoon as she heard the hum of the snowmobile and met Brady outside. Who did Brady ask to comfort him, play with him, listen to him? He seemed so alone, and she couldn't figure out why. He was a handsome, intelligent man who could have any number of women vying for his company. He was also a complex man, and she knew better than to try to understand him . . . but she suddenly found that she wanted to very badly.

"Ready?" he asked, his half smile both boyish and appealingly adult. It made her stomach flip-flop.

Putting on her gloves and zipping her key into her pocket, she walked around and examined the trailer on the back of the snowmobile so she didn't gawk at Brady. Clothes on or clothes off, he was the most masculine man she'd ever been around. "How big is this tree going to be?"

"At least ten feet. I have a particular one in mind." He motioned to the saw tied to the trailer. "But don't worry. You don't have to help me cut it down. It's a one-man saw."

"And here I thought I'd have a chance to build up some muscles."

His lips twitched and amusement danced in his eyes. "You don't need muscles. Not when everything you've got is exactly in the right place."

He paused, then flushed slightly, looking as embarrassed as she was astonished. Heat flooded through her until she thought she'd have to shed one of her layers.

Closing his eyes, he grimaced. "Sorry. That sort of slipped out. I guess I'm a bit rusty in the compliment category. I didn't mean it as a come-on."

The quick flicker of desire she'd caught glimmering in his eyes before he'd closed them made her want to ask, "Didn't you?" But she was afraid of his answer and she didn't want to spoil the afternoon. "The compliment is gratefully accepted," she murmured. "Rusty or not, it was nice."

Again that flash of hot desire he quickly quelled. "You're an attractive lady. I'm surprised some fine Texas gentleman hasn't snapped you up."

She wondered if he was as interested in her as she was in him. The thought both excited and scared her. "Is that a question?"

He gave a lazy shrug. "An observation."

She bit back a smile. "I see. Well, I guess I haven't given any fine Texas gentlemen the opportunity to find me. I'm pretty busy and I do a lot of traveling to teach and lecture.''

"No social life?"

"Oh, yes. I don't know what I'd do without my friends. We go out most weekends when I'm in town. Theater, concerts, dancing at clubs.''

He hitched his thumb in his front jacket pocket. "Your life is filled with people, isn't it?''

"I like it that way. I was alone a lot as a kid." Uh-oh. She shouldn't have said that.

"With a brother and a sister?''

Her blond, blue-eyed sister now modeling in New York had never wanted a not-so-acceptable Abigail tagging along. "Connie's three years older. She's always had her own interests. Kent's five years older and was usually involved in sports. He was off to college when I was twelve." She added softly, "But he was always there for me when I needed him.''

"Did you need him often?''

Remembering Kent's protective arm around her when other children made fun of her still warmed her heart. "When the world got too difficult for me to handle on my own. What about you? Who helped you through rough times?''

Brady's restless steps toward the snowmobile signaled his lack of willingness to discuss his personal life. "I always had my father. And I had a best friend. Cole. We went to high school together, played football, worked in movies together.''

"He's a stuntman, too?''

"He was killed doing a stunt.''

Abigail's heart stopped. "I'm sorry. Were you working together?''

"I was with him.''

The four words said so much and so little. What had happened? Had this tragedy made Brady such a loner? She hesitated to ask a question about something that obviously caused him pain, but she wanted to know more, she wanted to know him. "Is that when you gave up stunt work?"

"Shortly after. A lot of things happened at once." Gesturing to the snowmobile, Brady closed the subject. "Let's get going. Hopefully I can attach the lights to the tree while everyone's at dinner so the guests can help decorate it this evening. Dad likes to make it an occasion."

"What about you?"

"Occasions come and go. Life goes on." Brady climbed onto the machine first.

Abigail stepped on the running board and swung her leg over the seat. "Do you put a star on the top of the tree?"

"Yes."

"Do you sing Christmas carols?"

"Along with serving hot cider and Christmas cookies."

"Then it's an occasion I don't want to miss."

Brady looked over his shoulder, intensely studying her face, searching for something.

She smiled. "I love Christmas, Brady. I love anything that brings people together and makes them realize they're all connected somehow."

He seemed to absorb that, then primed the engine and squeezed the handle to move them forward.

The trail they blazed over loose powder took them behind Brady's log home. Abigail held the grips on the sides. If she leaned forward just a few inches or so, her chest would press against his back. She wondered if her arms would even go around him, he was so big.

He picked up speed over an expanse of pure white snow and her knees bumped against his thighs. Even through his ski suit she could tell they were built, hard, strong. The same way his arms were. Remembering his bare chest, the curling hair that invited her fingers to stray through it, she let go of the grips and leaned a little closer.

As they covered the clearing and entered a grove of evergreens, the snowmobile lurched and Abigail's arms slipped around Brady to steady herself. She felt him tense and she didn't know what to do. The floor of the forest was uneven; it was safer to hold on than to let go. Resting her right cheek against his jacket, her arms not quite meeting at his waist, she closed her eyes for a moment.

To be able to hold a man again, to love a man... Tears pricked in her eyes. Why did outside appearances always make a difference? What if she had come to the lodge without makeup on her face? Would she be here with Brady now?

Experience told her *probably not*. Hope and a dream said *maybe he's different*.

Brady brought the snowmobile to a stop and didn't move. Neither did she. Her breathing seemed to match his and both of them were breathing faster. The forest slipped away; so did the snow and cold. All she thought about was holding Brady.

Then he lifted his hands from the controls of the snowmobile and the movement straightened his spine. Abigail leaned back and took her arms from around him.

Hopping off the machine, Abigail sank into the snow. Brady swung his leg over the seat and jumped off. After he untied the saw from the trailer, he straightened. Smiling, he approached her and held out his hand. "Walk in my footsteps or I'll have to dig you out."

She took his hand; his grip was firm and strong. "You told me I wouldn't have to ski. How about a pair of snowshoes?"

"We don't have far to go." He backed up, waited until she stepped into his prints, then let go. He started off but tossed over his shoulder, "If I go too fast, yell."

She didn't have to yell because every few seconds he glanced back to make sure he wasn't leaving her behind. Finally he said, "Listen."

Only the wind flowing through the tall pines with a muffled shifting sounded in the stillness. "What am I listening for?"

"The quiet. The peace. The softness of silence only winter and snow can bring."

"I suppose this is why tourists come here. It's a world away."

"A lifetime away."

The husky distance in his voice made her ask, "What brought you here, Brady?" She wanted to know more about him, to figure out why a handsome, interesting man was hiding himself away.

"I wanted to start over. To begin again."

"What did you leave behind?"

"That's personal, Abigail."

"Or does it hurt too much to talk about?"

His sunglasses hid his eyes, but she felt his gaze bore through her. "You ask too many questions." His flat intonation signaled annoyance, maybe even anger.

Taking off her sunglasses and hoping he'd do the same, she responded, "Only when I care about the answers."

He turned away and stared at the treetops. "Maybe you care too much."

"In other words I should mind my own business. I suppose I should. But I've found the more someone keeps something bottled up inside, the more it hurts and damages. It's amazing what light does, Brady."

"Light?"

"The light of day, the light of sharing."

Brady took off his sunglasses and slid them into a pocket. His austere frown spoke of pain he wouldn't share. "Light hurts as much as memories. It makes the truth glaring, and the guilt unbearable."

Guilt? What kind of guilt was he carrying? "Guilt drags us down, Brady. It doesn't change the present or the future."

He lifted his head and angled away from her so she couldn't see his eyes. "And what could you possibly know about guilt? You give people their lives back. I doubt if you know anything about destroying them."

"I can't believe you destroyed anybody's life."

His thick brows raised at the certainty in her voice, and she knew he hadn't expected her to challenge him. "You don't know me, Abigail. I should have acted when I didn't, I should have considered someone else's fears to be more important than my need for kicks. I deserve the guilt."

She stepped toward him then, not caring that there were no footprints to help her, not caring when she sank in above her knees. "And the sadness, too?"

Reaching out, he cupped her chin. "Don't care so much. It's dangerous."

His voice was as deep as he was masculine. "For you or for me?" she asked softly.

He slid his thumb across her chin, his touch sending a slash of heat to her face and a tingling through the rest of her. "For both of us."

"I thought stuntmen thrived on danger."

"They know when the amount of danger is worth the risk and when it's not. *If* they know what they're doing."

"And you know what you're doing."

"I know what I have to do."

"What?" She waited, needing his answer, dreaming of his kiss.

"I have to cut down a Christmas tree." He withdrew his hand. "Do you think you can hold the trunk while I saw?"

She blinked, the switch in conversation and the change of mood throwing her off balance. He'd gone from intensely intimate to cool and casual in a matter of seconds. He was good! And she had a feeling his defense mechanisms were more expert and practiced than hers could ever be.

"I'm stronger than I look, Brady. Holding up a tree won't be a problem."

He accepted her response with a lift of his brow, his green eyes teeming with mysteries he wasn't ready to reveal. "Then let's go get it. It'll be dark soon."

Abigail suddenly understood Brady knew everything about darkness, but nothing about light.

Chapter Five

Abigail held the tree while Brady sawed. After a few minutes, he stood straight. "Okay. Let go and step back so it falls to the side." When the tree hit the ground, he motioned to the way they'd come. "Walk back in my footprints. I'll drag the tree to the trailer."

She watched as he hefted the tree onto the trailer as if it were as light as a log, then wound a rope around it and the saw. "It's going to take a lot of decorations to fill that tree."

He smiled. "And even more lights. With everybody helping, it shouldn't take too long. I don't suppose you could convince Theodora to join us."

"If you stop at her cabin, I'll try."

With night falling, and remembering the bumpiness of the forest floor, Abigail braced her hands on either side of Brady's waist. He didn't tense up as before, maybe because he expected her hold this time.

Stopping at Theadora's, he waited while Abigail knocked on the door. As expected, the actress declined the invitation. Abigail hopped back on the snowmobile. "She's getting closer to wanting my help. I'm hoping tomorrow she'll let me evaluate her."

"It would be a nice Christmas present for Dad if she does."

Wanting to know more about Brady the man, not the tough-guy image he projected, Abigail asked, "What do you want for Christmas?"

"Santa Claus hasn't visited me for a while."

"If he decided to stop this year, what would you like?"

Brady shrugged. "I don't need anything, Abigail. I'd probably wish for Luke to accept Sheila and his father being together, or maybe Dad setting aside his old-fashioned views so he could have a life with Theadora."

Abigail didn't know many people who would give up a wish of their own to help someone else—even in their imagination.

A few guests stood in the lobby as Abigail held open the door for Brady when he carried the tree into the great room.

Unzipping his jacket, he said, "You ought to go to dinner."

"What about you?"

"I'm going up to Dad's place to change. I'll grab something from the kitchen after I wrestle this into the stand."

She didn't want the interlude with Brady to end, but she knew it would simply because they were back at the lodge. "Thanks for asking me to go along. I enjoyed it."

He took off his jacket and threw it over a chair. "It's beautiful country."

"I enjoyed the company, too."

His green eyes became opaque and she couldn't tell if he was sorry he'd asked her along or not. "You'll have plenty of company tonight."

"Who puts the star on top?"

Brady's lips twitched. "Do you want the honor?"

She smiled. "Kent and I used to fight over who'd put it on. But Connie usually won without saying a word."

Brady turned toward the tree. "I'll let you know if you have to compete for the job. I doubt it."

Abigail got the distinct feeling Brady wanted to end the conversation. Not wanting to be with him if he didn't want to be with her, she stuffed her gloves into her pocket. "I'll see you later."

Before she reached the desk, Brady was already adjusting the tree stand. Apparently he'd asked her along this afternoon as an apology for his suspicions. And that was that. She should be relieved.

Trying to feel relieved, she went to dinner.

Brady changed into a sweater and jeans, then grabbed a sandwich in the kitchen. He didn't look for Abigail as he passed through the dining room, but not doing so was an exercise in self-discipline. He seemed to gravitate toward her like the proverbial magnet...or like a sun-starved plant reaching for the light. He wished what she'd said about light was true. But he wasn't willing to experience pain to find out.

Brady had built the tree stand especially for a tree this size, so putting it in place didn't take long. After winding yard after yard of white twinkle lights around the evergreen, he was finally satisfied. By the time he'd hauled boxes of decorations from the storage room to the great room, guests had begun to wander about, or stop to talk and watch.

He had one more trip to make. Wondering why Abigail hadn't arrived yet, he announced to those milling around, "If you want to start decorating, feel free."

When he came down from his dad's apartment, he saw why Abigail had just trailed in. His gut churned as she and Stover headed for the crock of hot cider, their heads close together as they conversed. Brady would bet his snowmobile they'd had dinner together again.

Refusing to recognize his jealousy, he told himself he was concerned Stover would take advantage of Abigail. Swallowing that rationale for the time being, he noticed Abigail seemed oblivious to him as he spoke with guests, supplied a step stool for higher levels of tree decorating and munched on one of the chef's oatmeal cookies. Not once did she glance his way.

She was wearing her hair clipped on the right tonight. His fingers curled into his palms. Her hair always looked so soft, so silky. . . .

Stover casually draped his arm around her shoulders, and Brady moved. Not a minute too soon, judging from the sounds of it.

"You could come to my cabin for dinner tomorrow," Stover was saying. "We can order lobster, chocolate mousse, champagne. . . ."

Brady could imagine exactly where Stover planned to serve all that. In his bed. He closed his hands into fists.

Abigail had been aware of Brady when he'd walked through the dining room. She'd been aware of him as he moved from guest to guest while Jim Stover had tried to charm her to his cabin. Brady's tan fisherman-knit sweater looked soft and comfortable, his shoulders capable of holding the world. Yet, she wondered if he'd already supported it for too long.

Brady stepped close enough to touch her. "Are you ready to attach the star?"

She slipped away from Stover and her arm brushed Brady's. Stover's gesture of familiarity had made her feel creepy. Touching Brady, him touching her, made her feel . . . right. "Do you think the step stool is high enough?"

The barest smile slid across his lips but didn't look as if it belonged there. "We'll manage." Taking her by the elbow, Brady guided her toward the tree. "Sorry if I interrupted."

Right. He'd come charging over like a bull out of a pen as soon as Stover touched her. She smiled. "Tell me one I'll believe."

The intent of arguing passed across his face; then he grinned. "Did you want to have a tête à tête with Stover?"

"No. That's why I let you intrude."

His brows arched. "You 'let' me?"

"Do you think I would have allowed you to pull me away if I was interested in him?"

Brady almost growled, "You're too friendly."

"Brady, men like Stover think they have to try or they don't feel like men. To tell the truth, you kept me from having to bruise his ego."

"I'd like to bruise more than his ego," Brady grumbled, raking a hand through his black hair.

Could he be jealous? A small thrill ran down Abigail's spine. "Why?"

He looked taken aback for a moment. "I've seen him take advantage of women."

So, Brady wasn't jealous. He simply had an overblown sense of responsibility. "He can't take advantage of me if I don't let him."

"You can't be charmed?"

"Not by Jim Stover."

Instead of continuing the conversation, Brady went over to the desk and picked up a box. Taking off the lid, he lifted out a three-dimensional gold star. Abigail held out her hand and he laid it across her palm. "The wire on the back slips over the top branch."

"I'm ready if you are." Their gazes connected and Abigail suddenly wondered if she *was* ready, if Brady could accept...

Brady hooked the leg of the step stool with his foot and dragged it toward the tree. "You're right. This might not be high enough. Do you want me to do it?"

She climbed the three steps. "Not a chance." When she leaned forward, the stool started to tilt.

Brady clamped his boot on the bottom rung and held her at the waist. "Go ahead. I've got you."

His large hands almost circled her waist and she froze, not knowing if she'd ever breathe again. The warmth of his fingers steamed through her sweater.

"Abigail? It's all right. I'll make sure you don't fall."

Stretching toward the top branch, she slipped the wire over it. The pressure of Brady's hands increased on her waist. She felt grounded, secure. Once the star was attached, she turned toward him. Taking his hands from her middle, he offered her one to balance herself as she stepped down. She took it, more for the chance to hold it than for the support. When she stepped to the floor, they were so close, she could tell that the casual part of Brady's hair was as natural as his full black beard. She could see a small scar on his forehead, tiny lines at the corners of his sensual mouth. He smelled male, with a hint of soap and the outdoors.

"I thought you might like some cider," Jim Stover said, startling her. In his hand he held two mugs.

"Thank you." Searching for a topic of conversation that would include both men, she said, "The tree looks wonderful. All that's left is the tinsel."

Brady nodded toward the boxes of the gold decoration sitting on a chair. "You can have the pleasure if you'd like."

"Or we could go back to my cabin like we discussed and play a game of backgammon," Stover interjected, looking at Abigail, making her wish she'd never agreed to have dinner with him a second time.

Brady was staring at her curiously, and she knew he was wondering if she would agree to Stover's plans. "I understand Christmas carols are planned next. I wouldn't want to miss them. And after that, Jim, I have some work to catch up on."

He frowned. "I thought this was your vacation."

"A working vacation. It's the only way I could manage a month off."

"Are you working tomorrow afternoon? We could take the shuttle to Crested Butte...."

"Abigail's agreed to go tobogganing with me tomorrow. Haven't you?"

She jerked her head toward Brady, her eyes widening. He couldn't have surprised her more if he'd hit her over the head. Rescuing again, was he? "You *did* say you'd show me the original Pine Hollow. We got sidetracked the other day."

Brady's brows lifted and a hint of a smile played on his lips. "Did I say that?"

"Mmm-hmm. About the same time I said I'd go tobogganing."

He nodded as if she'd scored a point. "Let's see if you're as good at throwing tinsel as attaching stars."

"Are you going to help?"

"Nope. I'm going to provide the music for the Christmas carols." And with that, he left her at the tree with Stover.

Abigail was learning quickly that Brady was a man with many facets. As she watched him cross to the desk, she felt Stover's gaze on her.

"I didn't know you and he had something going," Stover said, taking the box of tinsel from her hand.

"Oh, but we don't. We're—"

"I saw the way he looked at you." Stover chuckled. "I wouldn't mind having his job. Practically every week he has a new load of guests to keep happy. It's a helluva way to meet women. Sure beats the bar scene."

Abigail's emotions protested, *No, Brady's not like that.* But her mind told her Stover could be right. What did she really know about Brady Crawford?

A few minutes later, the host of the lodge surprised her again. She had thought he would set up a stereo system...or something. The "or something" was a folk guitar in his very capable, large hands.

Abigail forgot about hanging tinsel on the tree as Brady captured her attention. Maybe it was the sight of him, sitting on the stool, guitar propped on one long jean-clad leg, fingers leisurely strumming, his black hair dipping over his brow as he looked down at his fingers. Maybe it was the sound of him, his deep baritone sure and clear as he started "Deck the Halls" and called for everyone to join in. Maybe she couldn't look away simply because of Brady himself.

Ethan came to stand beside his son and joined in, encouraging other men gathered to sing along, too. Abigail didn't know how many carols they sang—ten, perhaps twenty, because she was fascinated by the hint of a smile on Brady's lips, the rich texture of his voice, the sparks in his green eyes when he caught her watching him.

He ended the concert with "Silent Night." As guests clapped and murmured to each other, Brady packed the guitar in its case and propped it at the desk.

Abigail felt him approach and started teasing tinsel across the branches. "You have a great voice."

"It's adequate."

Draping her last strand of tinsel on the tree, she argued, "It's more than adequate. The guests enjoyed you and the carols." She thought she saw a flush creep into his cheeks and wondered why compliments embarrassed him. Or was it *her* compliment?

Ethan called, "Everybody stand back. Let's light it up." Stooping over, he plugged in the extension cord. A thousand stars blinked behind wooden sleighs, gleaming balls, cherubs and bells. Although the star on top wasn't electric, it reflected the bouncing light and sent it back out over the tree.

A hush went over those gathered, then someone began applauding. Abigail joined in. "It's beautiful."

Brady smiled. "This one does have a particular appeal. But I still like the ones standing in the forest best."

Abigail glanced out the window, then went toward it and pushed back the curtain. "It's snowing."

"We're supposed to get five inches by morning."

She sighed. "I should get back to my cabin."

"I'll walk you back."

"That's really not necessary, Brady."

"You don't want company?"

"Company's fine. I just don't want you to think you have to protect me."

"From Stover?"

"From anyone," she answered definitively.

"All right. I'll just walk along beside you, then. If the Abominable Snowman jumps out from behind a tree and tries to snatch you, I'll let him."

She laughed. "You've got a deal."

Abigail went to the coat rack for her jacket. Brady disappeared, then returned with his. When he opened the French doors, she preceded him outside.

The deck glistened with a powdering of snow. Flurries drifted through the floodlights, gracing the wood with a fairy-touched sheen. The frosted tips of trees, still heavy with the last snowfall, towered over the cabins.

Abigail's fingers itched to sketch the scene. She'd already done one of the lodge and one of the remembered view from the top of the hill where they'd skied. Every scene here was more perfect than she could imagine it.

Carefully descending the steps, Abigail looked up at Brady beside her. He was gazing ahead, tall and straight and sturdy. He belonged here. In some ways, she saw he didn't want his solitude interrupted. Yet, there was something about Brady that spoke of city and culture rather than woods, refinement rather than coarseness.

The first blush of snow on the path made it slippery. As her heels dug in, Brady grasped her elbow. Their silence on the way to her cabin was more comfortable than not. Most of the guests of the cabins had plugged in the electric candle that sat on the sill in the middle of the sitting room's window. Abigail had remembered to light hers and it beckoned like an old friend.

At her door, Brady turned to her. "You don't have to go tobogganing with me tomorrow."

"I want to" slipped out before she could think of a less eager way to say it.

His half smile made her knees wobble. "We'll take the snowmobile, but we will have to drag the toboggan back up to the top of the hill each time."

"I haven't had any more signs of altitude sickness. I did an aerobic workout yesterday and today, and I didn't have a problem."

"Good."

He was staring at her mouth, and she couldn't keep from staring at his. Would his beard be soft or coarse, his lips firm or softly seductive?

He tipped up her chin and ran his thumb lightly over its point. "You'd better go in. The temperature's dropping."

Not for her. Her body was heating up. Should she invite him in? If she did, would he think...

"Abigail, do you know you're more tempting than Eve? And I'm damn tired of resisting."

He waited a fraction of a moment, long enough for her to protest, back away, agree he should resist. But she couldn't do any of those things because she wanted his kiss as much as she wanted to be held in his arms.

When he bent his head, she closed her eyes and felt the heat of him, the surprise flash of delight, the simple caress of lips touching lips.

And then it was over. All too soon. Her mind didn't even have time to register the texture of his beard; she felt cheated.

"You *are* still resisting," she murmured, dazed by the complex emotions the light kiss stirred.

"Maybe I have more sense than Adam," he returned in a rough voice, stepping away. "Good night, Abigail. I'll see you tomorrow."

He'd dismissed her, but there was a caring in his voice that she suspected he didn't want to feel. So she accepted his dismissal. "Good night, Brady." Opening her door, she went inside. As she peered out her cabin window, she watched Brady walk back toward the lodge. That quick touch of his lips hadn't been nearly enough. She wanted more. A lot more. Heart racing, emotions swirling, she considered the consequences of becoming involved with Brady.

Unzipping her jacket and shrugging out of it, she went into her bedroom and picked up the sketch pad on the chest. As she had for years, she would make sense of her emotions with lines and shading, shadows and light. She would turn herself inside out on paper, and then she would know what to do.

Abigail was getting used to the snowmobile as a mode of transportation. She was also getting used to sitting behind Brady, her hands braced on his waist.

There'd been no mention of last night's kiss. But she wasn't surprised—she could feel Brady's caution as tangibly as her own.

Brady drove the snowmobile alongside his house, then veered to the right. After a few yards, he pulled into a circular clearing.

Over his shoulder, he whispered, "Look at the ground around the trees."

The snow appeared untouched at first glance. But then Abigail spotted tiny claw prints, pronged indentations from birds lighting on the surface. As she and Brady sat in the silence, she heard small scratchings, flutterings not belonging to the tree branches.

"I attach feeders in these trees and bring food for anything not hibernating. This is my Pine Hollow. Whether or not it's the one the lodge was named for, I don't know. I come down here to think. You should see it in spring and summer when the wildflowers bloom and the scent of pine is so strong, you can taste it."

"This is a special place," she murmured. Somehow, whispers and murmurs seemed appropriate here. Looking up at the vibrantly blue sky, she tried to imagine the clearing at night. "I bet you can count every star, and the moon drapes a path across the center."

"When it's full," Brady said, immediately picking up on her train of thought.

Abigail glanced around the clearing again and thought she saw a glimpse of something furry. Then it was gone.

A short while later, Brady drove them to the top of a hill where the sun was so glaringly bright, Abigail blinked behind her sunglasses. At breakfast, she'd learned they'd received four inches of new snow. Out here, everything looked untouched, as if it had been clean and pure and there forever.

Brady took the toboggan from the trailer.

"I didn't expect it to be made of wood. Plastic or fiberglass, maybe."

"This one's made from strips of hickory."

Abigail ran her hand over the curved front. The undersurface of the toboggan had a high polished gleam.

"Frontiersmen used toboggans to transport their game home. The first ones were made of bark." Brady slid the toboggan into position at the crest of the hill. Beckoning to her, he said, "You sit in front. Back passenger steers."

Abigail climbed on, her feet braced against the curved wood. As Brady took his position, she held her breath. Somehow, he pushed them off and settled himself behind her, his long legs on either side of her. She barely had time to register the sensation of his huge body against hers as they plummeted down the hill. Her stomach flip-flopped, the wind singed her cheeks, the speed amazed her. The downward force pushed her against Brady or was it him against her? It didn't matter. She was surrounded by him. That was as exciting as winter's answer to a roller-coaster ride.

As they coasted to a stop, the toboggan tipped slightly over a low hill. Abigail sat perfectly still for a moment. So did Brady. Until she heard his deep voice at her ear, his warm breath caressing her cheek.

"Well? What do you think?"

She looked over her shoulder. "I think I want to do it again."

He laughed—a real laugh that turned up his lips in a full-fledged smile. "We'll see how often you say that after we've trudged up the hill."

Abigail soon lost count of the number of times they zoomed down the hill and pulled the toboggan back up. She insisted Brady let her drag the toboggan, too, and although it took her twice as long, he let her.

With each speeding journey down the hill with Brady, Abigail became more comfortable with his arms around her holding the guide rope, with his thighs brushing her knees. The toboggan tracks zig-zagged across the snow. Sometimes they forged a new track, other times they coasted over a previous one.

Brady pushed off in a direction that made a new track. As they picked up speed, Abigail realized they were gliding faster than before. The toboggan skidded a little, as if the terrain underneath were icy. At the bottom of the hill she heard Brady swear. She swayed against him as the toboggan fishtailed, tumbling her over.

"Abigail, are you okay?"

She was sitting a few feet away from him and the toboggan in the snow. "I think so."

Immediately he was by her side, helping her up. "I couldn't steer it over the icy patches."

Brushing loose snow from her arms, she laughed. "I'm surprised it didn't happen sooner."

Brady tipped her chin up. "Look here."

Not knowing what he was going to do, she met his gaze. He ran his finger below her temple. "You must have hit the toboggan. You have a few scratches. It already looks as if it's bruis—"

She stepped back so quickly, she stumbled. Brady cupped her elbow. "Abigail, I'm sorry. I didn't mean to hurt you."

"You . . . you didn't," she stammered, keeping her hand at her side so she didn't rub her makeup off if there were scratches. What he thought was bruising might be her birthmark.

"We ought to go back and put antiseptic and ice on it. We can stop at my place."

"No."

"No?"

Her gaze slid away from his. "I mean, that's silly. I'm fine."

He reached toward her again. Ducking, she searched in the snow for her sunglasses and found them next to the toboggan. "I am getting cold, though. Maybe we should go back." As she brushed off more snow from the front of her jacket and put on her sunglasses, she felt Brady's stare.

She should tell him right now. What did it matter if he knew?

What did it matter if he *didn't* know?

She shivered, and the moment passed. There was nothing to speak of between them, except a kiss that could hardly qualify as one. Except for the way it made her feel.

Brady scooped up the rope and righted the toboggan. She trudged up the hill behind him.

Brady hung the keys to the snowmobile on the rack inside the shed. When the door to the small outbuilding behind his house opened, he turned, thinking Luke might have arrived early again.

But Ethan came in instead. "I saw you taking Abigail back to her cabin. You two have fun?" His father's voice was calculatingly casual.

Brady took a chamois cloth from a shelf and wiped down the snowy nose of the machine. "I thought we were. I'm not sure what happened."

"What do you mean?"

Brady stopped rubbing. "We had a spill and she scratched her forehead. But when I suggested we come back to my place for first aid, she backed off like a frightened deer."

"Maybe she thought..."

"That my intentions weren't honorable?"

"Were they?"

Brady paused. Abigail was so friendly, so natural, so...everything. That simple kiss had been anything but simple for him. His body had responded instantly. She made him feel and think and wonder. It was the feeling that felt the strangest and was uncomfortable to boot. "I thought they were. But after we were back here... Who knows?" He went back to wiping down the snowmobile.

Ethan came closer. "You do. You'd never do anything a woman didn't want you to do."

Brady and his father had talked honestly about sex and women since Brady was twelve. "It's been a long time, Dad, and Abigail..."

"Is a pretty lady."

"It's more than that. She has this way of looking at things."

Ethan took in his son's posture, the agitated movement of his hand. "I want to ask Theadora to have

Christmas dinner with us. I thought we could ask Abigail, too."

"You want a real Christmas this year, don't you?"

"Don't you? Don't you think it's time you stop blaming yourself for having bad luck?"

Brady jerked straight up. "Bad luck? Dad, Cole died because I wasn't paying close enough attention—"

"Cole died because he'd had too much to drink the night before and his balance was off. Face it, son. You couldn't stop him from falling off that train any more than you could stop him from drinking."

"He was sober that morning. I never would have let him up there if he hadn't been. I checked his reflexes. They were good."

"Brady, Cole was not your responsibility! His life was his life. Did you ever talk to his wife after the accident?"

Brady hadn't been able to do more than offer Cole's wife, Mary, his condolences. His own life had been in such an upheaval because of the accident. All these years, his father hadn't asked questions, had let Brady deal with the tragedy stemming from Cole's in his own way. "No. Mary was so grief-stricken . . ."

"Maybe you should," Ethan advised.

"What?"

"Talk to Mary."

Brady leveled a look at his father. "What good would that do? Cole's gone. She probably blames me as much as I do." As much as his ex-wife blamed him for the loss of their baby.

"Maybe, maybe not. But it wouldn't hurt."

"Next time I happen to be in L.A., Dad," Brady responded, knowing that wasn't planned anytime soon. He took a last swipe at the machine and threw the cloth to the shelf as the pause lengthened between them.

Finally Ethan asked, "So what about Christmas dinner? Should we include Abigail?"

"You can ask her, but that doesn't mean she'll come."

"Maybe we could decorate your place a bit tonight. What do you think?"

Even though Ethan was worried about Theadora, Brady knew his father liked having her here, liked dropping in and talking to her whenever he could. If his dad wanted a festive Christmas, Brady would help any way he could. He owed his father. Like most children, he always would. "I'll find us a tree. There were plenty of decorations left over last night."

"Maybe I could fetch a small one for Theadora, too. She doesn't get out of that cabin. It might make her feel better."

"Do you think she'll put up a fight about coming to my place?"

"Not if I tell her we decorated just for her and no one else has to see her."

"You want to get the trees now?"

"We could. I'll eat a quick supper with Theadora after we get back. Then we can fix up your place."

Brady flicked the keys from the rack.

"Sure you don't want to warm up first?" Ethan asked.

"No, I'm fine." Hopping on the snowmobile, Brady fit the key into the ignition.

Before he could turn it, Ethan commented, "Besides the tree, we should hang some mistletoe, too. Don't you think?"

The suggestion brought pictures to Brady's mind that warmed him up real fast. Mistletoe and Abigail Fox could be a very dangerous combination.

Chapter Six

An hour later Abigail sat across from Theadora at her small dinette table. "Have you made a decision?"

"Yes. I'm ... I'm ready."

When Abigail had reached her cabin earlier, there had been a note on her door that Theadora wanted to see her. Upset from the way she'd reacted to Brady, Abigail had gone to the mirror to examine exactly what Brady had seen. Two superficial scratches. The makeup had still been intact. What Brady had thought was bruising must have been the spot where she'd bumped her head. But the whole experience had told her one thing—she cared what Brady saw, and she cared what he thought about it.

So she understood everything that Theadora was feeling right now, all her fears and insecurities. "Then take off your hat and veil and we'll get started." Abigail held her breath, not knowing if Theadora would comply.

The actress hesitated. Slowly her hands went to the edges of the veil. Dropping them, she murmured, "Abigail..."

"It's all right. Trust me."

After a moment, the older woman reached for the top of the derby and dragged it off quickly. It plopped to the table in front of her. Theadora lifted her chin and her regal bearing contradicted her trembling fingers.

Abigail reached over and took the actress's hand, staring into her beautiful hazel eyes filled with fear and dread and a tiny spark of hope. "Relax, if you can. I want to study your face. What did you get Ethan for Christmas?"

Theadora's lips formed a nervous but wry smile. "I have to be careful. He won't accept much."

"So you didn't buy him a Jaguar?" Abigail teased as she evaluated and objectively studied the actress's face.

"A truck would be more to his liking, and I'd give him the best money can buy. But, of course, he won't let me. So I have to be more creative."

"I suppose after all these years of friendship, you know what he enjoys."

"I think so. I got him a few little things, like a gold belt buckle with Pine Hollow engraved on it, and a new Stetson he probably won't wear until this one gets scrubbier. But I did manage something special. He collects stamps. A friend of mine who lives in France heard about a stamp collector's estate sale. At the auction he purchased a rare Australian something-or-other for me. Ethan should be thrilled. And the best part is he'll never know what I paid."

As she spoke, Theadora relaxed somewhat. She was a beautiful woman, blessed with a graceful forehead, high cheekbones, a patrician nose. On the right side of her face, she had three small scars on her forehead and two just below her ear. They were almost smooth and covering their rosy lines should be no problem. The two-inch scar on her cheek, which had been so deep it had needed a skin graft, was a different matter. It was dark, the ridges on either side of it smooth and shiny with no pigment.

Abigail sat back and crossed her arms on the table.

"What's the verdict?" Theadora asked hoarsely, betraying her nervousness.

"I think you'll be amazed with what we can do. And I'd like you to consider wearing your hair down around your face rather than pulled back."

Her hand went to her chignon. "I've worn my hair like this for years!"

Abigail smiled. "I know. But I think you'll see a big difference if you try it down."

Doubts rushed across Theadora's face.

Abigail nudged gently. "Do you want to talk to Ethan without the veil between you?"

A tear fell along Theadora's cheek. She whispered, "Yes."

That was all Abigail needed. "Then let's get started." Abigail opened her bag of cosmetics. Giving Theadora a tube of moisturizing cream, she directed, "Apply this all over your face. The makeup will adhere better."

Abigail had been careful to keep her skin moisturized at the higher altitude so her makeup looked as smooth and flawless as any model's. Yes, she always wanted to look good. But here, it was so important Brady look at her as he would any woman—with admiration and respect. Not with pity, or worse yet, with the repulsion she'd seen on Stan's face. She couldn't bear to see that disgust on Brady's face, she just couldn't.

What if Brady knew about her face? How *would* he react? Did she have the courage to find out? On the other hand, why should she tell him? After a few weeks she'd never see him again. Theadora didn't realize how lucky she was. She already had Ethan's acceptance whether she'd admit it or not.

After the actress finished with the lotion, Abigail explained each step slowly, blending shades on the back of Theadora's hand, smoothing the makeup on the older woman's scars, adding ivory for a lighter blend, using a thin brush to paint strokes. After waiting for the sealing powder to set, Abigail applied a water-based makeup over the scars and the rest of Theadora's face. The actress restlessly shifted on her chair.

Abigail played up Theadora's eyes with gray liner and a shading of muted gray on her lids with a wedge of green at the corners. Brown mascara brought out the rich hazel of her irises. A sweep of blush on her cheeks and peach lipstick on her lips enhanced her natural beauty.

Abigail laid the lipstick brush on the table. "We're finished. I have a hand mirror here, or we can go into the bedroom."

Taking in a deep breath, Theadora responded, "Let's go into the bedroom."

Abigail went in first and turned on the overhead light. Slowly Theadora walked to the dresser and switched on the boudoir light there. She peered into the mirror, then took a step back. Moving closer again, she tentatively touched the scar on her cheek.

"I don't believe it," she murmured. "I mean, you can still tell there's something there, but the ugliness is gone. I look...I look...almost normal." She stepped back again, farther this time.

"Can you take your hair down?"

Theadora's gaze met Abigail's in the mirror, then her fingers started on her chignon. Pin after pin dropped onto the dresser until she ran her fingers through her hair. Sweeping the brush through a few times, she let the blond waves fall around her face. Then she peered into the mirror again. "My goodness, it does make a difference!"

"Your cheeks are less exposed and the point of interest is your eyes."

"You're an artist!"

"My parents let me take lessons because they didn't know what else to do for me when other children shut me out. Drawing and mixing colors became my special world. When I became interested in cosmetology, I just carried over the ideas."

A sharp rap on the door startled them both. "Ethan," Theadora murmured and went into the living room. Out of habit she reached for her hat.

Abigail put her hand on Theadora's shoulder. "This might be a good time to forget the veil."

The actress patted her hair, ran her finger lightly over the scar on her cheek. "I don't know if I'm ready. What if he—?"

A second knock hit the door.

Abigail encouraged softly. "This is the way you look now."

"And if I want more than friendship with Ethan, he won't put up with the veil. Not that man."

Abigail suppressed a smile at Theadora's fond exasperation as the actress tossed her hat on the table and went to the door.

Ethan stood there holding a three-foot evergreen on a small wooden stand. When he saw Theadora without her veil, he gaped.

"Well?" she asked breathlessly.

His face broke into an ear-to-ear grin. "Dorie, you look wonderful. It's so good to *see* you again."

Abigail saw the tension leave the older woman's shoulders as she stepped back so Ethan could come in.

He looked as if he'd just won the lottery. Setting the tree on the floor near the window, he turned around. "If I stare, it's because I haven't seen you for so long."

Theadora's eyes grew shiny. "I feel . . . a little naked. As if my protection's gone."

"Dorie, you don't need protection from me. You should know that by now."

"But how will I look to outsiders, to my fans?"

"What does it matter?" Ethan asked impatiently.

"You know me better than that, Ethan. It just does."

"Maybe it's time your fans don't come first."

Abigail felt as if she didn't belong here now. Crossing to the table, she left the cosmetics Theadora would need and packed the others in her bag.

Ethan came over to her. "Thank you."

She smiled and closed her bag. "No thanks are necessary. Theadora, will I see you at breakfast?"

The actress shook her head. "I'm not ready for that yet. I don't know if I ever will be. You and Ethan are one thing, the public is another."

"What about Brady, Theadora? Will you feel comfortable with him? He wants me to invite you and Abigail to Christmas dinner at his place," Ethan explained.

"Brady's a friend," Theadora answered. She looked around the cabin. "It will be nice to have a change of scene. Especially for Christmas."

"And you, Abigail?" Ethan asked.

Picking up her jacket, she wondered whose idea this was. Was it truly Brady's? Half of her cautioned her to decline, the other half wanted to see Brady again badly. "That will be lovely. I can't believe tomorrow is Christmas Eve."

"It sneaks up." Ethan took her jacket and held it for her. "Are you coming over to the lodge tomorrow night? There's a shuttle that takes folks to church services. When they get back, we serve a late-evening buffet. It seems everyone smiles a lot more and is extrafriendly on Christmas Eve."

She slid into her jacket and zipped it. "That sounds nice. I want to make calls to my family first, but I'd like to join everyone."

"Shuttle leaves at seven."

"Do you and Brady go?"

"I usually do. But this year I'd rather spend the time with Theadora."

The look he gave the actress was filled with more than friendship. Abigail picked up her bag. Someday, she hoped a man would look at her like that. Then she'd know she was loved.

* * *

Christmas afternoon, Abigail stopped at Theadora's cabin to check the actress's makeup before they trekked to Brady's house. She'd spent the morning before teaching her how to mix the makeup and apply darker and lighter strokes with a brush for the desired effect. Theadora had learned quickly but was still nervous about doing it herself.

They arrived at Brady's around four. Ethan opened the door with a huge smile. "Merry Christmas, ladies! Come on in." He moved into the living room and motioned to the sofa.

Theadora preceded Abigail inside. "It feels so strange to be out without my face covered."

"Your hair looks lovely down."

Theadora's smile was radiant. "Ethan likes it like this."

"I sure do. Let me take your coats. Brady's in the kitchen basting the turkey."

Abigail hadn't seen Brady since they'd gone tobogganing. He hadn't been around at the buffet last night. She wondered how he'd spent Christmas Eve.

She'd wanted to give him something for Christmas, a thank-you for inviting her to dinner. The scrolled paper in her hand wasn't much, but she hoped it would show her appreciation and tell him... What? That she wanted to spend more time with him? A shiver skipped up her spine and she knew she was playing with fire.

After Ethan took her coat, she looked around the room. The other day when Brady had been barechested, she hadn't paid attention to anything else. The house emanated the same rustic ambience as the lodge. A six-foot Christmas tree stood in the corner by the staircase. Evergreen boughs lay across the split-log arches of the doorways. A forest-green leather couch faced the river-rock fireplace. Two other chairs with the same green and sky-blue tones sat on the side with an oak pedestal table between them. The coffee table was oak, also. A tall brass lamp shed a circle of mellow light while the blazing fire sent its warmth through a black mesh screen across the stone hearth.

The dining room beyond was small, with a round table set for four and flanked by four captain's chairs. Tantalizing aromas floated through both rooms from the kitchen. Still feeling embarrassed from the way she'd run from Brady, Abigail took the scroll and her courage in hand and headed for the kitchen.

Brady slid the roaster into the oven, closed the door, turned toward the counter and saw Abigail. A Christmas present with beautiful auburn hair, a figure in cream-colored slacks and sweater that begged for his hands' touch, blue eyes that could rival the endless depth of the ocean, and a shy smile that started his heart hammering in his chest.

Maybe he hadn't really believed she'd come and that was why he was so inordinately glad to see her. "Merry Christmas. Welcome to my corner of Pine Hollow."

"Merry Christmas to you, too." She crossed to him and held out something tied with a shiny green ribbon. "I thought if Santa Claus passed you by again this year, you needed at least one unexpected gift to open."

Her expression was vulnerable and open and if he'd ever wanted to kiss her before, he couldn't imagine wanting to kiss her more than at this moment. "You didn't have to bring anything."

"I know. That's the fun of Christmas."

His fingers touched hers when he took the rolled paper from her hand. He let them linger and slid their tips across her palm. Her eyes lit brighter than his Christmas tree, and he savored the awareness of heat spreading through him.

Untying the ribbon, he laid it on the counter, more than a little curious about the present. Slowly he unrolled the heavy paper. The sketch of the lodge captured everything he loved about it—the rough pioneerlike exterior, the mounds of snow, the aspens and pine framing it, their elegance stating they'd stood tall for decades.

He looked at her and didn't quite know what to say. "This took a lot of time."

"It's what I do to relax."

His eyes held hers. "You're very talented."

"I've been drawing since I could pick up a pencil," she explained lightly, though he noticed the pulse at her throat was speeding as fast as his.

"I'll have it framed and hang it in the living room. Thank you. I guess I was wrong about St. Nick passing by this year."

The silence grew between them.

Abigail's gaze slid from his as her hand fluttered at the stove. "Anything I can do to help?"

He drew in a breath, smelling not only turkey, but the tempting scent of Abigail's perfume. "How are you at mashing potatoes?"

"I haven't had much practice lately, but I'll give it a shot."

Reluctantly, Brady turned away from her, rolled up the sketch and laid it safely on top of the refrigerator. "I don't think Dad will be much help now that Theadora's here." Crossing to the stove, he lifted the pot of boiled potatoes and with the lid drained the water into the sink. "I guess you know he thinks you walk on water."

"Pardon me?"

Brady glanced at her. "The difference you've made with Theadora. I don't think she's touched that hat once in the last two days. At least not around us."

Abigail moved toward the counter, where the mixer was located. Her hair swung against her cheek, and he longed to touch it, to touch her. "She just needs to build her confidence now."

"I think Dad might be able to help her with that."

"I'd like to get her out with people."

"She's afraid they'll recognize her and stare."

"I know. But eventually she'll have to realize they're staring because she's famous, not because of her scar."

Brady dumped the potatoes into the mixer bowl and set them in place on the stand. "They're all yours. I have milk warming on the stove and the butter is in that white holder."

Abigail stood by the mixer and added a hunk of butter to the bowl.

"Abigail?"

She lifted her head. "Yes?"

"What happened the other day?"

She appeared flustered for a moment, and her eyes darted away. "I . . . uh . . . guess after spending the afternoon with you I realized how much I like spending time with you."

"So you ran away?"

Her gaze met his and he saw the turmoil there, though he had no idea what was causing it. "There's something you don't know about me, Brady, and—"

"You're married?"

"No."

"You're an ax murderess?" he teased.

She let out a little puff of air. "No. It's something that affects—"

He couldn't keep his hand at his side. Reaching out, he stroked her hair behind her ear. Responding to his touch, she trembled and he felt the same quivering response within his chest. "We all have our secrets, Abigail. Things that hurt too deep to put into words. But I don't care about your secrets. I like spending time with you, too. I haven't wanted to be with a woman in a long time."

Be with a woman. The word conjured up pictures for Abigail that meant more than an afternoon skiing or tobogganing. Even though Brady was now wearing a soft gray chambray shirt with his jeans, she could see his bare chest in her mind's eye, imagine his skin meeting hers... And what would happen when he found out about her birthmark? He said he didn't care about her secrets. She'd never thought of it as a secret, and she really didn't want to make it one now.

"You'll only be here a couple more weeks, Abigail," he continued. "And I'm not naive enough to believe distance makes the heart grow fonder. So when you leave...we'll probably never see each other again."

"So...what are you saying?" she asked, her mouth going dry.

"I'd like to enjoy your company while you're here. Making snow angels is a lot more fun when two people do it together."

The idea of playing in the snow with him made her grin. "And that's what you want to do? Make snow angels?"

"Among other things." His sexy half smile made her stomach do loop-de-loops.

Brady was being realistic about their situation. He liked living here, being isolated. She worked in Texas and loved being in the midst of people. What harm could there be in enjoying the next few weeks with him? "We can take each day as it comes and just...see what happens," she suggested.

He dropped his hand to his side, but the heat of his touch remained. "That sounds good to me."

"I looked for you last night," she confessed.

Brady propped his hip against the counter. "I spent the evening with Luke and his family."

"I'm glad. No one should be alone on Christmas Eve."

"Did you spend it with Stover?" The edge to his voice said he cared if she had.

"No. Somehow I don't think a Christmas church service is his cup of tea."

"But it's yours?"

"Things like that remind me how grateful I am that I have the life I do—family, good friends, work I love."

The timer on the stove buzzed. Brady tore his gaze from hers, pushed himself from the counter and switched it off.

With shaky fingers, Abigail lowered the mixer head and started the appliance. These few minutes alone with Brady had made her realize one thing. If she wasn't very careful, she could lose her heart.

Abigail couldn't remember a holiday dinner she'd enjoyed more. Theadora regaled them with stories about her acting career. Ethan told comical anecdotes about the stars he'd chauffeured. And Brady... Every once in a while he'd send her one of those smoldering looks that made her quiver with excitement.

Everyone helped clear the leftovers away and store them. Then Ethan offered to walk Theadora back to her cabin. After Brady assured the actress he'd see Abigail back to hers, Theadora accepted Ethan's offer and they left.

Brady took the sketch Abigail had given him and stretched it open on the bare dining room table. "Do you paint, too?"

Alone with Brady in the quiet house, Abigail felt a bit skittish. "Not as much as I'd like. I can't seem to find the time. I brought along my watercolors, but I haven't gotten to them yet."

He studied the sketch again, lightly smoothing his thumb over her signature in the corner. "You'd love painting here in the summer. The fields of wildflowers, the mountains, the hiking and bike trails through Gunnison National Forest. The scenes are breathtaking."

Brady's shirt hung loosely over his sinewy arms. He hadn't fastened the top two buttons and dark hair swirled across his tan skin. Abigail swallowed. "I think winter is pretty spectacular. How did you make the decision to settle here?"

"I'd been here on location for a movie one winter, then came back in the summer to do some backpacking. Carol wanted to try it—"

His abrupt stop cautioned Abigail to proceed slowly. "I guess I should ask you if *you're* married."

"*Was* married. Past tense. Ancient history."

"A divorce?"

"Seven years ago."

Abigail had so many questions. Was he still in love with this Carol, his ex-wife? Was she the reason he isolated himself here? What did his past have to do with his present? Brady's strained expression kept her from asking any of them.

He broke the awkward tension by asking, "Would you like some brandy?"

"A little. It'll warm me up for the walk back."

"Go ahead into the living room. I'll get it."

Restless, Abigail stood in front of the fireplace and admired the stonework leading to the ceiling. She heard a cabinet close in the kitchen.

A few minutes later, Brady came in and set the glasses on the coffee table. When she turned around, he smiled and crooked his finger at her. "Come here."

She followed him to the high archway between the living room and dining room, where he stopped. He pointed above them. In the boughs of green nestled a few sprigs of mistletoe tied with a gold ribbon. Her heart raced.

Brady nodded toward the sketch on the table. "I don't have a present for you."

"I didn't give you one so you'd give me one in return."

"I know. That's probably why I want to. Some presents are just less tangible than others."

"What ... did you have ... in mind?" The question came out much bumpier than she intended.

"This," he murmured as he bent, and his lips drew near to hers.

He gave her plenty of time to back away if she didn't want his gift. His green eyes pierced hers as he paused, waiting. She didn't want to back away. She wanted his lips on hers and his strong arms around her. So he'd know, she swayed toward him.

Passion flared dark and hungry in his eyes a split second before his lips finally met hers. She didn't know his arms had encircled her until she felt the gentle caress of his hand on her back. Lifting her arms around his neck, she realized his beard was as soft as his hands were gentle. Captivated by the texture of him, she laced her fingers in his thick hair while she relished the firm, persistent heat of his lips and the caress of his beard against her chin. Closer. She needed to be closer.

When her breasts met his chest, the kiss changed. He opened his lips and slid his tongue along the seam of her mouth. More. They both wanted more. Opening to him, she accepted the sweet invasion of his tongue. A trembling began that rippled through her like a fiery wave, making every nerve ending come alive, magnifying every sensation.

His hair slid through her fingers, his arms enclosed her tighter, his tongue explored, heightening sweep after sweep of desire coursing though her. His jeans rubbed against her wool slacks, his thighs against hers, his shirt against her sweater, his chest against her nipples. She'd never expected to feel so much. She'd never expected to want to give him all she was with one kiss.

Everything was in the kiss—passion and fire, freedom and fear, hunger and need. It was the peak of the mountain and the bluest Colorado sky. It was the pureness of snow and the fierceness of ice. Tears came to her eyes because it was everything she ever wanted and maybe everything she couldn't have.

Abigail felt Brady's groan shudder through his body as he deepened the kiss, feverishly stroked her back, and pulled her to him to cup her bottom. She knew she was lost and didn't know why, knew she cared for Brady too much already, knew that ending the kiss and any time with him could break her heart. And still she gave... dreaming and hoping and praying.

Brady told himself it had been a long time since he'd kissed a woman this way, told himself Abigail couldn't possibly taste this sweet or feel this soft or be more arousing than any woman he'd ever taken to bed. And that was straight where this kiss could lead. To bed. To heaven... or hell... or heartache. Did either of them want that? With no promises? With no future? With Abigail not knowing the kind of man he was? That he'd cost himself and his wife their baby?

An icy blast of wind from outside couldn't have made logic reign over passion any faster. He broke away, dropped his arms and tried to control breathing as ragged as his emotions.

Abigail swayed and he caught her by the shoulders, but as soon as she balanced herself and opened her eyes, he let her go. He knew he couldn't sit beside her on that couch, sip brandy, and not want to lay her down, strip off her clothes and take her with all the demand, need and arousal he'd felt since the first time he saw her.

Gathering every ounce of control he possessed, he didn't wait for her reaction. "Brandy on the couch in front of the fire could be a very bad idea," he warned her, part of him hoping she'd disagree, the other part attempting to be noble and realistic and unaffected by her scent, her softness and the turmoil she evoked.

Her gaze darted to the staircase that led to the bedrooms. For a moment she hesitated, then moved away from him. "I'd better leave."

If she didn't, he was afraid they'd both have regrets. "Abigail..."

She turned away quickly and headed for the closet. "Holidays can be more tiring than the longest workday."

Pushing her away was easier and safer than letting her in. So he didn't contradict her. "I'll walk you back."

Opening the closet, she pulled her coat from the hanger. "That's not necessary."

"To me, it is. I want to make sure you get back safely." He was trying to keep both of them safe.

Evading his eyes, she shrugged into her coat. "All right. If you insist."

"I insist," he said more curtly than he intended.

The explosion of passion between them had changed the camaraderie of dinner, the anticipation of spending time together, into something much more incendiary, tender, serious and awkward. It was definitely time to regroup and decide exactly what he was ready to give. And take.

Chapter Seven

Snow fell as Brady sat in his home-office the day after Christmas, trying to keep his mind on bookkeeping. But Abigail's face kept appearing before him, her passion-filled eyes, her lovely smile. He'd told her he didn't care about her secrets. That hadn't been nobility; it had been selfishness because he didn't want her poking into his. He couldn't get involved with Abigail without telling her what had led him here.

The phone rang, and he picked it up, grateful for the distraction.

"Brady, it's Lou Feeney. How are you doing?"

Lou had trained Brady in stunt work at the beginning of his career. He'd seen Lou now and then when he was shooting. "I'm doing fine. Surprised to hear from you."

"I have a proposition for you."

A sense of excitement stirred Brady's blood as he thought about going back to L.A. and the work he'd left. "I'm listening."

"I hear you're making a comfortable living from the lodge."

"Did you get hold of my tax records?"

Lou chuckled. "I've got my ways. But I thought you might be interested in doubling your income."

Money didn't mean as much to Brady as to some people. He knew it couldn't buy peace or happiness. "And you know how to do that?"

"Remember when Gus Solomen stayed at your lodge last summer?"

Gus had been an acquaintance from L.A. who'd produced an award winning action-adventure film the year before. "Sure, I remember."

"We want to turn your lodge into a training camp for stuntmen."

"You've got to be kidding."

"I don't kid about money and moviemaking, Crawford. You're sitting on a gold mine. The perfect area to train stuntmen winter and summer. Trails and forests and fields. And a mountain nearby for skiing. But on top of it all, you can get back into the swing and coordinate the whole shebang and give young guys your experience. You're the best, Crawford. We're not turning them out like you anymore."

Brady let the compliment pass. "You want me to sell the lodge to you?"

"Not necessarily," Lou drawled. "There are several ways we could work it. Bottom line is Gus and I would be your partners in the training camp. Why don't you come to L.A. and we'll discuss it?"

Brady ran his hand over his beard. "Give me some time to think about it."

"That's better than an out-and-out no. While you're thinking, imagine getting rid of your mortgage, making plenty of money and doing work you love. I'll be in touch if you don't call me first."

Brady hung up the phone and stared at it for a moment. Getting back into stunt work, teaching it. Could he? Did he want to?

Living here had made him quiet. In L.A. he'd never been the party sort. But this isolated life had made him withdraw into himself. He knew that. He didn't miss the publicity hounds, the actors or the directors. But he did miss the stunts, and the lights and the sets—the work itself.

The doorbell interrupted Brady's ruminations. He shut down the computer and went to the door. When he opened it, he found Luke. Brady grinned. "What are you doing with yourself since you're off for Christmas vacation?"

The teenager shrugged as he came in. "This and that. Can we take out the snowmobile?"

"Your dad's still isn't fixed?"

"Nah. He's thinking about getting a new one. But in the meantime, I've got nothing to do."

Brady glanced toward his office, then out the living room window. "I could use a break." Maybe the cold air would clear his head and he could make a decision about Abigail and the lodge.

After riding a groomed trail for the better part of an hour, Luke took off his helmet and pointed to an open field. "I'll hop off. I want to see you take it over those moguls. Can you jump them?"

Brady smiled as adrenaline pumped at the thought. "I can try. But I'll do it under one condition. You don't attempt it. You have to be trained in case something goes wrong."

"Yeah, yeah. I know. You've told me often enough. I'm ready to take off for L.A. right now and get started."

"One more year, Luke. Then you can consider it."

The teenager hopped off the machine and planted his feet wide apart. "I'm gonna do it, Brady. I'm gonna get out of this town and see something other than ranches and skis."

Brady made sure the safety catch was secured to the ring on his glove. If he tugged or fell off, the snowmobile's engine would shut off. "You might be disappointed, Luke. Big cities have their drawbacks, too."

Luke frowned. "Maybe. But I wanna make up my own mind, not have someone make it up for me. Once dad and Sheila get married, I won't fit in here at all. Any place'll be better than here."

Brady knew, at this point, that nothing he could say would change Luke's mind. Only experience would teach him.

Revving up the snowmobile, Brady sprayed snow and took off toward the first mogul. As he sailed over it in a mist of white powder, he remembered the thrill of taking chances and felt alive once again.

Abigail couldn't find Brady anywhere. Their kiss had shaken her and apparently it had affected him, too, because he wasn't on her doorstep asking her to make snow angels with him.

Late in the afternoon, needing fresh air and a stretch for her legs, she bundled up against the cold and went for a walk. Before she knew it, she was headed for Brady's house, but not his front door. Hiking along the side of the house in the tracks of the snowmobile, she noticed a few flurries beginning to fall. Another hour and it would be dark.

The hollow was as silent as it had been the first time she'd seen it, until she stopped and listened. Then she heard the drone of a voice, a voice she recognized. Walking forward, she saw a flash of black by a row of aspens. She didn't think about *not* going to Brady.

He was tying a bell of seeds onto a low branch. As she approached, she heard a flutter of wings. "I didn't mean to scare anything away."

Brady glanced at her, then put his gloves back on. "They'll be back."

The silence was broken only by the sound of her breathing. "I'll leave if you want to be alone."

His eyes met hers. "No. I think I've been alone enough."

She took a few steps toward him. "I enjoyed yesterday, Brady."

He frowned. "So did I."

"You don't sound happy about it."

"You've stirred up my life, Abigail. I'm not sure I like it."

"I see." She shouldn't feel hurt, but she did. And some of it must have laced her words.

Brady stepped closer, reached out and took a strand of her hair between his fingers. "No, you don't. I've buried a lot of feelings. At least I tried to. But burying isn't the same as erasing. That kiss yesterday hit hard, and I can't let something that honest happen again without you knowing the truth about me."

Abigail had associated with scores of people over the years. Everything about Brady spoke of honesty and strength of character. "What is the truth?"

Brady looked to the top of the trees. "I married when I was twenty-nine. I was financially secure, had a good reputation among the producers and directors for my work. But Carol, my ex-wife, hated what I did. She was constantly afraid something would happen to me. The longer we were married, the more she clung. She wanted me to quit. It became an ongoing argument. All I knew was stunt work. To appease her, I took a few business-management courses, but I knew I wouldn't use them until an injury or old age kept me from the work I loved."

"She wanted you safe."

His brows drew together as he frowned. "Her idea of safety bored me to death. I couldn't imagine being cooped up in an office eight hours a day."

"Then why did you quit?"

"Carol got pregnant and her fears escalated. I checked in three or four times a day to reassure her, but she didn't want me out of her sight."

Abigail could imagine the claustrophobic atmosphere that created for Brady. "You felt trapped."

He nodded. "Big-time. Work became my escape. And then the accident happened."

"Your best friend?"

Brady's gaze slipped away from hers to the expanse of white behind her. "Yes. I felt...feel responsible for what happened."

"Why?"

"*Because* we were friends. Cole was living the high life, drinking too much. That's lethal in my business. I tried to make sure he didn't work unless he was sober and one hundred percent. But that day..." Brady dug his hands into his pockets.

Abigail didn't want to pry but she suspected Brady needed to release the pain he still carried. "What happened?"

"We were cutting a train sequence, running across the cars. We were filming in almost slow motion as we always do in those kinds of scenes. The camera was undercranked and the train moved slowly. But for some reason Cole lost his balance. I was right behind him and I reached out to grab him, but I wasn't quick enough...."

"Brady," she whispered.

He looked at her then, his eyes tortured. "It was a freak fall. He broke his neck. Carol heard about the accident before I could get to her, and she thought I was the one fatally injured. She miscarried our baby."

"Brady, it wasn't your fault."

Scowling, he disagreed. "Of course it was. If I had quit, if I'd found another line of work..."

"She still could have miscarried."

"That's unlikely."

"Why do you have to carry all the blame?"

His sigh was a white puff of air. "Because nothing worked out right. After the miscarriage I did quit. Dad and I bought this place, and Carol and I tried to put our lives back together. But she longed to be back in California with her family. The bottom line was she couldn't forgive me. And I couldn't forgive myself."

His green gaze pierced her. "Now do you understand what kind of man I am? I couldn't put my wife and child first, so they were taken away from me."

Her heart ached for him, for his loss and for the heavy weight of guilt he carried. "You really believe that?"

"Yes."

"Brady, if you had quit stunt work and taken a job you hated, wouldn't you have resented Carol? Wouldn't that have affected your marriage, too?"

His tone was impatient. "I don't know. But certainly you of all people can understand Carol's side. You don't like stunt work any more than she did."

"That might be true. But I also know you can't be happy with someone else until you're happy with yourself."

"I could have compromised, moved out here sooner...."

She dared to ask, "Would you have been satisfied with that? Would your wife have liked it any better?"

His answer was slow in coming. "I don't know."

Abigail couldn't keep from touching his arm, from wanting to heal his hurt and his sadness. "You can't punish yourself forever, Brady."

"Is that what I'm doing?" he asked seriously, as if he hadn't considered it before.

"It looks like it."

He gently ran his finger across her lips. "I don't know if I'm ready for you."

The suede glove on her skin was soft and warm. She closed her eyes to savor the sensation of his touch. "I don't know if I'm ready for you."

As he moved closer, she opened her eyes and saw the fire in his. "A few weeks, Abigail. That's all we have."

"I know," she murmured.

He lifted her chin and when his lips met hers, she knew she wanted as much as he was prepared to give. She'd told herself she didn't need a man in her life. And she didn't. But Brady wasn't just any man. He was a special man. His touch thrilled her, his kiss aroused her, his strong arms held her and made her feel safe and secure. What was it about him that cried out to her? What was it about her that felt the need to answer?

His mouth covered her lips possessively with a hard demand that hadn't been there before. She held tightly on to his shoulders so her world stayed balanced. Brady surrounded her with his arms, his hard sinewy strength locking her against him until there could be no distance between them. The padding of their jackets was an unwelcome cushion, a distracting barrier that kept her from Brady's heat. Her gloves prevented her from touching him.

Wriggling off her glove, she searched for someplace she could touch and found the hot skin of his neck. Working her fingers under his wool cap into his hair, she sighed in delight. He took advantage of her parted lips and speared his tongue inside. With a thoroughness that took her breath away, he swept her mouth.

He drew away for a deep breath but came back to her a moment later. As his hand brushed up and down her back, she arched into him. He groaned and erotically rocked his hips against hers. He was fully aroused and she knew if they didn't slow down, she'd be in his bed before the sun set. That wasn't what she wanted. Not this soon. Maybe not at all. She had to tell him about her birthmark first. She had to be as honest with him as he'd been with her.

Going against her body's cry for more, she pulled back. Taking her arms from around Brady's neck, she braced her hands against his chest.

He swore and held her shoulders. "You make me forget we're standing in snow and it's only twenty-five degrees. I'm sorry. Let's go into the house."

"No," she whispered.

His brows arched. "No?"

She slid her hands away from his chest, letting them drop to her sides. "Brady, this is happening so fast. And I'm not sure..."

"That you want to do more than make out?" he finished with a hard edge to his voice.

"I'd like us to get to know each other," she said softly as flurries of snow floated from the gray sky.

"We're not kids, Abigail. I want you, and I don't play games."

"No games, Brady. That's the point. I'm not...I don't..."

"Have an affair every time you go on vacation?" he asked in a low voice.

She couldn't tell if he was angry, annoyed or simply trying to understand. "I haven't taken a vacation in five years. I've been too busy."

"And what about when you're *not* on vacation?" he asked with a tilt of his head.

"I'm busy then, too," she murmured as a snowflake landed on her nose.

"And you don't fall into a man's bed without giving it a lot of thought."

"I don't fall into men's beds, period. Brady, I've been serious about only one man, and..."

He searched her eyes and her face. "He must have hurt you badly."

"We hurt each other." If Brady asked her how, she'd tell him what happened. She'd also tell him she was still a virgin.

But he didn't ask. "I don't think being alone in my house or at your cabin is a good idea if you simply have talking in mind. How would you like to go to a play in Crested Butte tonight?"

"I'd like that. But can we get tickets this late?"

Brady smiled. "I know the owner. Do you think we could convince Theadora to go along? No one will know her or expect to see her."

"It could be the exact kind of outing she needs. If we both ask her and Ethan does, too, we can probably override her objections."

Brady picked up her glove from the crust of snow where it had fallen and handed it to her. "Then, let's do it. While I still believe there's safety in numbers."

They started walking toward the cabins, and Abigail wondered how long they could surround themselves with people. And how long they could be alone, kiss and not give in to more.

Theadora fidgeted during the drive to Crested Butte. Abigail glanced over her shoulder and saw Ethan take the actress's hand and tuck it between his.

At the theater, when no one recognized Theadora or stared, she relaxed. But Abigail's nerves became strung tight. Seated next to Brady, his arm or leg brushing hers whenever he moved, she became much too aware that he was a very virile man and she responded strongly to the sound of his voice, his scent, the simplest touch of his hand.

As they stood in the back of the theater after the play, Brady suggested they stop at a local pub.

Ethan objected. "Theodora probably won't like Mountain Ridge. It's not what she's used to."

"And just what am I used to, Ethan Crawford?" Theodora asked.

"Champagne, caviar and Spago's. Mountain Ridge is basically a country bar."

"You don't think I can enjoy something *you* might enjoy?"

Abigail exchanged a knowing look with Brady.

Ethan's brows almost disappeared under his Stetson. "If you want to try it, we'll go."

Several people called greetings to Brady as he guided Abigail to the rear of the pub with his hand on the small of her back. Garth Brooks's voice blared from the jukebox. Brady pulled out a ladder-back wooden chair as Ethan seated Theodora at the barrel-like table.

A waitress with a denim miniskirt and white fringed blouse came to take their order. As she was writing, she took a second then a third look at Theodora.

The actress finally asked, "Is there a problem?"

The waitress blushed. "I'm sorry. But you look familiar. I can't figure out..."

"Maybe I look like someone you know. I'm just visiting the area."

"Maybe." The girl gave a little shrug and went back to the bar.

Theodora touched her face. "She wasn't staring at my scar."

"No, Dorie. She was looking at you because you're beautiful," Ethan responded.

Theadora's smile was radiant as she covered Ethan's hand with hers.

A Clint Black ballad filled the pub. Brady turned to Abigail. "Would you like to dance?"

Abigail nodded, her heart leaping in her chest at the thought of being held in Brady's arms.

The dance floor was small. Only two other couples were dancing. Brady held out his hand to Abigail and she stepped into his arms. His grasp was firm yet gentle, his hold loose, as if afraid she'd break. Leading her in the traditional box, he said, "Dancing's not one of my developed talents."

She smiled. "I'll try not to step on your feet if you try not to step on mine."

She felt him relax as he brought her slightly closer. "Do you always know the right thing to say?"

"No."

"It seems like it. How did you get to be so good with people?"

She gave a small shrug. "Practice, I guess. In my profession I mostly listen and encourage."

His gaze searched her face curiously. "You're the most real woman I've met in a long time."

"Is that a compliment?"

He nodded. "Sure is. You don't duck, you don't hide."

"Brady, I need to tell you something. I—"

He brought her tighter against him. "You feel so good in my arms."

His voice floated around her, caressing her as his green eyes had. A voice whispered, *Tell him,* but a louder voice said, *A little more time won't matter. Take this moment and hold on to it.*

He brought her hand to his chest and smoothed his thumb over her knuckles. "What did you want to tell me?"

His hand on her back scorched through her sweater. His thumb on her hand created a rippling pleasure throughout her body. His shirt under her fingers, the scent of clean soap, his beard almost brushing her chin intoxicated her. "Nothing. Not now."

His nose grazed hers as he murmured, "Good thinking." He dropped the lightest of kisses on her lips, locked his hands at her back waist, and pulled her flush against him. All the air whooshed from her lungs as she laid her cheek against his shoulder and let his thighs guide their movement.

His lips brushed her ear and a shiver zipped up her spine. He must have felt it because he whispered into her ear, "You're a very sensual woman, Abigail Fox."

She lifted her head. "Are you trying to seduce me?"

Amusement mixed with passion in his deep green eyes. "Here? In the midst of this crowd?"

Several other couples had joined them on the dance floor, and most of the tables were filled. She wrinkled her nose at him. "I think I accepted a date with a wolf in sheep's clothing."

His amusement faded away. "My intentions are obvious. I want you. I'm not pretending differently."

His primal message was clear, and heat flashed through her. She turned her head and again laid her cheek against his shoulder. The music lulled her, but his hard chest against her breasts, his hips against hers, his arousal, which he didn't try to hide, excited her. Everything about Brady was controlled, restrained. Picturing what could happen if he unleashed his desire should make her run away from him, not toward him. But in a sense she'd been running since Stan had rejected her. It was time to stand her ground and meet her own needs as well as Brady's head-on.

Her needs dictated that she should be more cautious this time, listen to her intuition, but let common sense count, too. And her common sense told her it was too soon to fall in love.

When the ballad ended, Brady lifted his head. She gazed into his eyes and couldn't look away. There was longing there and sadness, and sparks of desire that lit her own passion. Someone jostled her shoulder, breaking the spell.

A man in jeans and cowboy boots slapped Brady on the back. "I haven't seen you for a while. Why don't you and your pretty lady join our line. Let's get this joint jumpin'."

Brady glanced skeptically at Abigail. "I don't know, Fred."

A twangy fast-paced song blared out and Abigail said, "Let's try it." At least if she had her mind on dance steps, she wouldn't feel so pulled toward Brady.

Brady shrugged and a line formed, crisscrossing the dance floor.

Fred led the group, showing them a pattern. Abigail watched carefully, trying to memorize the footwork. In a few minutes the music started and she looked at Brady. He was wearing charcoal dress slacks with a jade shirt. The sleeves flowed full, the rest of the material laid over his broad chest and back as if it had been custom-made for him. But even dressed as he was, he didn't look out of place. His beard, his rugged masculinity, his hello's to people he knew farther down the line, said he belonged in the midst of jeans, Stetson hats and tooled leather.

Abigail had thought the line dance would make her less aware of Brady. But she found herself watching him when she wasn't watching her feet. After she picked up the rhythm and the basic pattern, she couldn't keep her eyes off him. He was gracefully athletic, every movement precise and controlled. His shirt flowed over his muscles, molding to him more the longer they danced. His expression was relaxed and he looked as if he were truly enjoying himself. She always sensed a tension about Brady. It wasn't there now.

When he turned after a glide, he caught her watching him and grinned. She misstepped and almost tripped over her feet. Grasping her elbow, he waited until she caught up to the footwork before he let go. Then he resumed dancing as if he hadn't stopped.

The dance ended and beads of perspiration collected on Abigail's brow. Taking a tissue from her pocket, she dabbed gently, careful not to rub. Brady hung his arm around her shoulders and led her back to the table.

His damp heat surrounded her, and she wanted nothing more than to burrow into his chest, taste another of his kisses and touch more than the skin at his nape. Tamping down desire that was escalating into high gear, she swallowed hard and found her voice. "I thought you said your dancing talent wasn't developed."

"I suppose I should have qualified that. Couples' dancing is what I don't know—the waltz, the tango—more than what you and I were doing out there. I usually join in the line dancing whenever I come in."

As they passed a table, another man and woman greeted Brady.

"Do you come in often?"

"Usually every weekend."

"You're not the loner you pretend to be. You enjoy being with people, too."

He stopped and his eyes narrowed. "I don't pretend anything, Abigail."

"I'm sorry. Maybe *pretend* is the wrong word. You wouldn't seek out company or come here to dance if you truly wanted to be alone."

He'd taken his arm from her shoulders, and his stance was defensive. "Maybe I come here to pick up women."

She searched his face. "Is that what you want me to believe?"

"Maybe I don't care what you believe."

She'd pushed him into this conversation, so it was her own fault if what he said hurt her. Quick tears pricked in her eyes and she turned away so he couldn't see them. But she'd only managed a step when he clasped her arm.

"I didn't mean that."

She took in a breath. "I'm sorry I pried."

He raked his fingers through his hair. "I'm not used to having my behavior analyzed."

"I didn't mean to do that. I'm trying to understand you, Brady."

He capped her shoulder with his palm. "Is that so important?"

"Yes."

"Why? We're only going to be in each other's lives a few weeks. You don't need to know about my childhood. I don't need to know about yours. We've got now, Abigail. That's all anyone has because the future never turns out as we expect."

"The choices I make now determine my future."

The lines along Brady's forehead eased away and he gave her one of his half smiles. "Did anyone ever tell you that you think too much?"

She'd analyzed life, hers and everyone else's, since she'd been a child feeling as if she were on the outside looking in. Kent often told her she coped with her world by taking it apart piece by piece and examining it under her microscope. "My brother tells me that. But, of course, I don't pay attention to him."

Brady took her hand and walked her back to their table.

Ethan and Theadora had their heads close together in conversation. When they realized she and Brady had returned, they looked a bit sheepish.

Brady seated Abigail, then sat next to his father. "Are you two hatching a plot?"

Theadora's hand fluttered at her chest. "Us? Why ever would you think that?"

"Because you both look guilty as hell. Dad, what's up?"

Ethan smiled slyly. "Nothing you need to know about right now."

Theadora leaned close to Abigail and whispered, "I think you'll like what we're planning. I'll tell you all about it tomorrow morning. Come over after breakfast."

Chapter Eight

"A press conference?" Abigail repeated the next morning as she sat across the table from Ethan and Theadora.

"It's time I stop hiding." The actress patted her cheek. "I don't have to now, thanks to you. I told Ethan I wanted to do something special for you, and he suggested I make your work known across the United States. I can do that for you, Abigail. What do you think?"

"I'm not exactly sure what you have in mind."

"All I have to do is put out the word that I'm ready to give an interview, and we can have TV networks and the print media here in a matter of hours."

"But do you want to do that?" Abigail asked.

"Yes. I want to end the speculation about me, put rumors to rest and help you. What better way?"

Abigail thought of one very huge glitch. "Does Brady know what you're planning?"

Ethan looked concerned for a moment. "Not yet. We wanted to see what you thought first."

"I think it's a wonderful idea. So many victims don't know help is available. This will get the word out. But if Brady doesn't approve..."

"What can it hurt?" Ethan asked rhetorically. "If nothing else, it will promote business for the whole area."

"I don't know, Ethan—"

"Trust me," he suggested. "I'll take care of the arrangements with Brady. We'll provide a luncheon for everyone after the press conference."

"When do you have in mind?"

"Tomorrow," Theadora answered. "Before I lose my nerve or change my mind."

"You can do it that quickly?"

"I called my publicist this morning. She said she can have the word out within the hour, and she can fly in tomorrow morning. So, what do you say?"

Abigail thought of all the people she could reach with the publicity, as well as Theadora finally coming out of her self-imposed cocoon. "I say let's do it."

Sitting in the great room with the sheer curtain panel pushed aside, Abigail sketched the view from the deck. Maybe when she had time, she could capture the majesty of the mountains on canvas. For now, she had to be satisfied with pencil on paper.

Concentrating, she didn't hear anyone approach, so she jumped when she heard Brady's deep voice.

"You lied to me, didn't you? You do want to be famous. And Theadora is your ticket to success." He was clearly angry, his jaw rigid and set, his eyes hard.

She sighed. "Ethan told you about the press conference."

Brady's gladiator stance was emphasized by the combative tone of his voice. "Just what kind of manipulation did you use on Theadora and my father? Did you open those big baby blues and plead, or did you tell Theadora she should do this for her own good?"

Abigail set the sketchbook and her pencil on the floor beside her. "Do you always jump to conclusions?"

He slashed his hand through the air. "It wasn't much of a jump. I know how women manipulate. Carol did it constantly, making me feel guilty for doing work I enjoyed. If I was later than she expected, she accused me of not caring about her. If I had to go out of town for a shoot, she'd complain I wasn't putting our marriage first. I turned down a lot of plum jobs because of Carol, because I was trying to prove I loved her, because I felt so damn guilty. So I know how women manipulate for their own purposes."

She tried to keep calm. "This wasn't my idea."

"Sure," he bit out sarcastically. "An actress who's been hiding for three years suddenly wants to face the world. How stupid do you think I am?"

Abigail stood, hurt by his judgment of her and angry with his presumption she was like his ex-wife. "I don't think you're stupid, I think you're blind. You've been hiding away longer than Theadora. She's decided she's had enough. She's ready to face her public again so she can get on with her life. Why didn't you ask your father whose idea this was?''

"Because I didn't have to. He knows I don't want to turn this lodge into a three-ring circus. He knows I value my privacy."

"They're not coming to interview *you*," she reminded him. "Or is that the problem?"

"What do you mean?"

"Maybe you're not so removed from your former life as you think you are. Maybe you'd like to go back to it.''

"I'm getting too old. I know that," he snapped.

"That doesn't keep you from wanting to go back."

"Listen, Abigail. I've had an offer to turn this lodge into a camp for stuntmen. If I wanted to return to that life, I would have jumped on the deal."

"Here? They want your lodge?"

He grimaced as if he hadn't expected to divulge the information in that way. "Yes."

"Are you going to do it?"

"I haven't decided. But that's not the issue here. The press conference is."

"And you still think it was my brainchild?"

He didn't have to answer because she could see the suspicion still flickering in his eyes.

"You know what you're doing, don't you?" she asked.

"What?"

"You're trying to find reasons to keep me at arm's length." She shook her head. "You can think what you want about me. The truth is I'm excited about the press conference. It will be good for Theadora, and I'm thrilled I can get the word out to people who have no hope. And if you have an objection to either of those reasons, then you're the one with the problem.''

The turmoil in Brady's gaze, her urge to hug him, the hurt that he didn't trust her, all bombarded her. To escape the storm of feelings, she turned and walked toward the dining room. She wouldn't be able to swallow a bite of lunch, but she'd try. After she'd broken up with Stan, she'd told herself she'd never again let a man's rejection hurt her. But now she knew hurt was sometimes like love. She couldn't control it or prevent it. It just happened.

Brady stared at the sketchbook on his coffee table. He'd found it next to the chair in the great room of the lodge earlier this evening. He'd taken it to the dining room, thinking Abigail might be there. Instead, he'd learned that some of the guests had taken the shuttle to Crested Butte for dinner and shopping. One of the waiters had told him Abigail had been among them.

Lifting the sketch pad, he settled it on his knees and opened it. The sketch of the mountains was unfinished. Paging through, he encountered soft shades of snow on pines, the clear brilliance of a winter landscape at midday, a darker version picturing long evening shadows. Though he expected to see another landscape when he turned the page, the next sketch startled him and made his hands go cold.

The sketch was of him.

He studied the man on the paper. She'd captured him, all right, and he didn't like what he saw. It wasn't a picture of a happy man. She'd made his eyes expressive, the tilt of his mouth almost a frown. He looked like a man in turmoil, a man who'd been knocked around by life and hadn't yet found his place. How had she shown all that with a pencil and paper?

He'd misjudged Abigail from the beginning. Why? Because he was attracted to her? Because she was good and kind and sweet, and he didn't believe he deserved any of that?

Maybe because she was breaking down his walls, brick by brick. Damn right, he was trying to keep at arm's length. What would happen if he didn't?

He'd get torn to pieces again like he had after Carol left. Abigail wasn't here to stay. Not with her profession. And what if he turned the lodge into a camp for stuntmen? That would send her running away faster than his suspicions. He wasn't ready to give Solomen an answer, but he was willing to discuss it. He could fly to L.A. next week.

While Abigail was still here?

Hell, he didn't know. Nothing was simple anymore.

The dining room had been transformed under Ethan's management to a press briefing room. He'd told Abigail to stay with Theadora in the ski-gear storeroom until he came and got them.

Abigail paced back and forth, then glanced at Theadora, who was calmly paging through an issue of *Vogue*. "Aren't you nervous?"

Theadora's finely arched brows rose a notch. "If I'm nervous, it's because of the announcement I'm going to make."

"Announcement?"

She crossed her fingers. "Say a little prayer. I'm hoping this tips Ethan's hand and he realizes we can spend our lives together." Standing, she patted her hair. "Do I really look all right?"

"You look beautiful."

"I am a little concerned how the scar will look on a close-up. You can bet they'll focus in on it."

"You can use it, Theadora. Explain how you felt before you used the makeup and how you feel now. The camera won't pick up any more than your magnifying mirror did."

Ethan opened the door and beckoned them to the hall. "This is it, ladies. We've got the three major networks represented and papers galore."

"Have you seen Brady?" Abigail asked.

"Not yet."

"Have you seen him since yesterday?" She hoped this hadn't caused a problem between the two of them.

"Not since I told him about the press conference. He wanted nothing to do with it, so I made all the arrangements with Theadora's publicist and the staff here."

"He blames me for it."

Ethan shoved his hat back. "Do you want me to set him straight?"

Abigail shook her head sadly. "I don't think it'll make a difference."

"Brady and I don't talk as much as we should. Maybe we respect each other's privacy too much. But I've found when I push my son, he clams up."

"The strong, silent type," she muttered.

Ethan chuckled. "You could say that." He patted Abigail's shoulder. "He's a hard sell because he's had a tough time. But I think he's caring again about a lot of things because of you."

When the three of them entered the dining room, the buzzing of at least twenty-five voices rose in volume. Flashes went off. Theadora didn't even blink. Abigail's palms sweated.

Brady slipped into the back of the room, behind the rows of chairs, behind the reporters milling about. He watched his father direct Theadora and Abigail to the table in front, where a portable public address system was set up. The two women complemented each other. Theadora's pale pink lace dress, her blond beauty, made Abigail's purple-and-turquoise dress and burnished hair seem even more vibrant. As always, Theadora looked regal and composed. Abigail's eyes darted quickly from one corner of the room to another.

She saw him, and their gazes locked. Then Ethan pulled out a chair for her. She turned her head and didn't look back at Brady again.

Theadora's publicist spoke first. She told the press the actress would make a statement, then answer questions.

Theadora took the microphone and smiled at the group. "Hello, everyone."

"Why have you been hiding away so long?" one reporter called.

Another inquired, "Did you have two or three operations?"

"Is it true you're going to buy Pine Hollow as a getaway? Are you going to return to films? Is it true you've been offered a two-million-dollar script?" a woman in the second row asked in a rush.

Theadora's publicist grabbed for the mike, but Theadora shook her head and responded firmly. "Please hold your questions until we are finished.

Many of them will be answered if you're patient for a few minutes.''

The group quieted and Theadora nodded. ''Thank you. As you all know,'' she began, ''I was in an automobile accident three years ago. There have been tabloid stories about my disfigurement, stories that, while exaggerated, came close to the truth. Unfortunately, my skin has a tendency to scar and the plastic surgeon did what he could. He has suggested we try again, but I'm afraid that will worsen the problem.

''This is the first time I've appeared in public since the accident, and for that, I thank the woman sitting next to me, Abigail Fox. She has given me back my life.'' She paused, then continued. ''Because of my vanity, I will never appear in public without my makeup. But I can show you where I have scars.'' She traced her index finger over each one, ending with the line across her cheek. ''You can still see the remnants of the worst one if you look closely. I'm sure the cameras will pick it up. But believe me when I say the makeup makes all the difference in the world. Without it, I would not be sitting in front of you now. I'd still be hiding behind a veil, or locked away so no one could see me. That's why I'm doing this. Miss Fox and those like her have a remarkable talent, and I want anyone who is in the position I was in, of being afraid to leave their house because everyone would stare, to know there is help. Now I'd like Miss Fox to tell you in a little more detail exactly how she can help people like me.''

If Abigail was nervous now, Brady noted, she didn't show it. She spoke into the microphone with confidence and composure, explaining her credentials, discussing the type of makeup she used, how it could be custom-mixed by anyone once she taught them the basics. She talked about a few of the clients she had helped, showing before and after pictures.

After Abigail finished, Theadora was bombarded with questions. She laid to rest rumors, answering factually, not giving more information than was necessary.

Eventually, reporters directed questions to Abigail. She fielded them well, tactfully sidestepping any inquiries dealing specifically with Theadora, but she elaborated on all others that dealt with her work.

Finally the barrage subsided and became sporadic. Theadora again took the microphone. "I have one more bit of information to give you. But, I warn you, I will not answer any questions concerning it. During the lunch the lodge has so graciously provided, Miss Fox will be glad to discuss her work in depth with anyone who is interested."

The actress smiled at Abigail and winked. Then she said, "I'd like to announce that I am retiring from the moviemaking business. It has been kind to me, and now I intend to enjoy the fruits of my labors. Thank you all for coming."

Abigail's gaze met Brady's, and it showed understanding. They both realized Theadora had just freed up her life so she could spend it with his father. As a loud buzz rushed through the press, Brady glanced at Ethan. He looked stunned and not altogether pleased.

When the press rushed forward with their tablets, pencils and tape recorders, Ethan came to stand beside Theadora and her publicist like an overprotective bodyguard. A member of the group around them tried to edge closer to the actress. Ethan scowled and held out his hand like a stop sign. "You heard what the lady said. No questions.'' He pointed toward the buffet table. "Time for lunch."

Ethan's deep voice, his six-foot height and his stony expression dissuaded anyone else from coming near Theadora. He escorted her and her publicist down the hall and away from the commotion. Brady suspected his father and Theadora would be having a serious discussion over *their* lunch.

Ethan had told Brady he was going to shoo Theadora away from the ruckus after the press conference. He'd also asked Brady to keep an eye on Abigail as she spoke to the press and made herself available for discussion.

So Brady kept a watchful eye on her as she went through the buffet line engrossed in conversation with a blond woman reporter. As she sat at one of the round tables, those at the table with her kept her involved in conversation. Several others stopped and asked for business cards. Abigail had hers ready. Brady supposed there would be calls galore coming in for her in the next few days.

It took two hours for the room to clear. The last reporter who had waited for Abigail's undivided attention finally left. With her sketchbook under his arm, Brady approached her and sat beside her.

She looked up, her expression studiously neutral. "I looked for that yesterday. I was hoping you had it."

"I probably shouldn't have, but I looked through it,'' he confessed, feeling awkward but encouraged because she hadn't told him to take a hike. At least not yet.

"Did you?'' The quiet inflection made him feel guilty as hell.

"You've sketched a picture of a man trying to keep everyone at arm's length, not just you," he admitted.

She looked down at the stack of business cards the various reporters had given her. "Today was important, Brady."

"I realize that now. I guess I just didn't want to be invaded. This place has become a haven for me. I can keep the world out. You brought it in."

She glanced around the room to make a point. "They've left. All of them. Nothing's changed. Except more people know they can find help."

"You're wrong," he disagreed, unable to keep the husky note from his voice. "I've changed. I'm starting to feel again, and I don't like it one bit."

Abigail's eyes widened.

"Sex is one thing, Abigail. Caring *while* you have sex is another." From her silence, he could tell he'd shocked her. "You're such a lady. And so innocent in some ways."

The shock disappeared and angry silver sparks shot from her blue eyes. "Don't patronize me, Brady. I'm twenty-seven."

"And I'm forty. You've seen one side of life and become a compassionate woman because of it. I've seen another side and become suspicious instead."

Abigail ran her finger along the edge of the sketch pad. "So where does that leave us?"

"It's been leaving *me* waist-deep in hot water." His admission brought a small smile to her lips, which he had a decided urge to kiss. But the kitchen staff was still moving about.

"You're pretty good at swimming out of it," she responded softly.

His heart lightened, and even more than kissing her, he just wanted to hold her, to enjoy the sensation of having a caring, lovely woman in his arms. "Does that mean you'll make snow angels with me this afternoon?"

"I could be convinced," she answered with an innocent coyness that brought heat to very particular parts of his anatomy.

Tipping her chin up with his knuckles, he kissed her with a persuasive nibble and a flourish of his tongue that opened her lips on a soft moan. He stroked her cheek and ended the kiss much more quickly than he preferred. He didn't want to get carried away here. And he could very easily. Abigail awakened and stoked primal urges he'd suppressed too long.

"Convinced?" he asked, trying to control his ragged breathing.

"Yes," she responded in a whisper.

His emotions might be in an uproar, and his future uncertain. But he knew one thing for sure. Abigail Fox was a special lady and he wanted to enjoy her while he could.

Theadora joined Abigail for dinner that evening in the dining room. Abigail had stopped at the actress's cabin so they could walk over together. Determination settled over Theadora's face as they opened the door to the dining room. Some guests openly stared at the celebrity as she walked in, others took covert peeps.

As they hung their coats on the rack, Theadora said, "Once they get used to seeing me here, they won't stare. I've got to get used to being an ordinary person. Or more important, others have to get used to it."

Theadora couldn't be "ordinary" in a month of Sundays. "I was surprised when you sent the message you'd join me for dinner. Is Ethan busy?"

The actress frowned. "He's angry. He said I've known him long enough to know he doesn't like surprises. I think he's hurt I didn't tell him about my announcement before I told the public."

"Why did you make it a surprise?"

Theadora sighed. "I wanted it to have as much impact as it could. I was hoping he'd be happy, not sulking."

"Maybe he needs time to think about it."

As they crossed to the buffet line, Theadora remarked in a low voice, "We're both almost out of time and old enough to know it. He's just being a stubborn, frustrating male."

Abigail smiled. "He sees you as a glamorous celebrity."

Theadora sniffed. "Well, it's about time he sees me as a woman. I don't know what to do. I'd be content to live here with him the rest of our days, but I don't think he's even considered that."

"Maybe he needs to see you in a new light."

Theadora picked up a plate and served herself a helping of carrot salad. "I'm listening if you have any suggestions."

Abigail wondered how blunt she could be. As tactfully as possible, she said, "You dress beautifully, Theadora." The actress's peach wool slacks and matching cashmere sweater were picture perfect. "But look around at the other women here."

Theadora quickly glanced at the guests at the tables. She understood Abigail immediately. "Most of them are wearing jeans. Many of them sweatshirts."

She sighed. "And I look like I'm dressed for a photograph session."

Abigail nodded.

Theadora gave Abigail a quick once-over. "I don't see you in jeans very often."

Abigail's green corduroys and multicolored sweater were casual, but even she felt overdressed sometimes in the lodge's relaxed atmosphere. "Old habits die hard. While you dress for the public, I dress so no one can criticize. It comes from when I was a child with a birthmark that drew everyone's attention. I always tried to make everything else about my appearance perfect so people would notice that rather than my face."

Theadora shook her head. "So what are we going to do about it?"

"There are some great shops in Crested Butte. And a hair salon with a good reputation. What if we go exploring tomorrow?"

"But how will we get there? I'd like to surprise Ethan...."

Both of them remembered what Theadora had said about him not appreciating the unexpected. Theadora smiled slyly. "He'll just have to get used to a surprise now and then. I'm going to show him I can fit in here if it kills me."

"There's a shuttle that stops here every morning at nine to take guests to Crested Butte." Abigail grinned. "It's not a limousine."

"I'm thinking ordinary, remember?" Taking a spoonful of green beans, she asked casually, "How are you and Brady getting along?"

"Fine."

Theadora nudged Abigail's elbow. "That's what you'd tell your mother. Now tell me the truth."

Abigail chuckled and thought about the fun they'd had this afternoon playing in the snow. "I like him a lot. Maybe too much. But we're very different. And since I'm going back to Texas in a couple of weeks..."

"Would you consider not going back?"

Abigail's stomach jumped because she'd been avoiding the question. "My work is in Houston. I need to be in a hub where I can reach clients. I love it out here, but it's so remote."

"Is that a yes or no?"

"It's an I-don't-know."

"When are you seeing Brady again?"

"Tonight. He said he'd drop by around eight."

Theadora forgot about the food in front of her as she squarely faced Abigail. "Don't waste time like Ethan and I have. If you find love, don't let your work or anything else get in the way. Because you'll regret it always."

Abigail realized Theadora spoke from experience that had given her wisdom, but she didn't know if she could heed the older woman's warning.

When Abigail opened her door to Brady, snow was falling. He looked as if he were dressed for skiing rather than an evening in her cabin that she'd been having jitters about since dinner. She was going to tell him tonight about her birthmark. And if it didn't make any difference...

Smiling, he said, "Get your boots and jacket and scarf. I want to show you something."

"Outside?"

His smile widened to a grin. "Yes."

"But it's snowing!"

"It does that a lot here. We're used to it. Come on. Bundle up."

The tilt of Brady's head, the engaging expression on his face, led her to do as he directed. When she closed her door, he grasped her hand and squeezed it, guiding her up the path to his house.

Catching his excitement, Abigail didn't ask any questions. Intuitively she knew he'd planned something special. But she expected a bottle of champagne, or a walk to Pine Hollow, not a sleigh sitting in his driveway.

Luke stood next to the huge horse, holding its reins. Abigail rushed forward and ran her hand over the red vinyl interior of the two-bench sleigh. "Is this yours?"

"It's my dad's," the teenager explained. "He rents it for weddings."

Brady climbed in the front seat and offered his hand to her. She took it and climbed in beside him. Covering her with a wool blanket, he added a silver one on top that was very light.

Luke handed Brady the reins and walked toward Brady's house.

"He's not coming along?"

Brady clucked to the horse and jiggled the reins. "Do you think we need a chaperon?"

"I don't know. Do we?"

He wrapped his arm around her. "We might later. It's too cold to do this for long. But this is an experience I thought you'd enjoy."

"It's lovely. The winter version of a convertible."

He laughed and squeezed her a little tighter.

The black night enfolded her and Brady in a snow-frosted world where the only sound was the rattle of the harness. She couldn't tell Brady about the birthmark now. Later.

Abigail relaxed against Brady, snuggling into his warmth, enjoying every moment in case it might be the last.

Chapter Nine

One look at Theadora, and Abigail considered the shopping trip to Crested Butte a success. Because of the press conference and clips on the news the evening before, many people had recognized the actress. Most had pointed, been in awe, and afraid to approach. In the sportswear shop, all the salesclerks had asked for Theadora's autograph. The beautician at the salon had refused to take her charge card, insisting that styling her hair was an honor.

Theadora had nudged Abigail and grinned broadly. "I like it here."

When they'd returned to Pine Hollow, Theadora had insisted she wanted to show Ethan the "new" her immediately. At the store, she'd changed into the clothes she'd purchased. Abigail walked beside her to the desk to see if they could locate Ethan or Brady. One would lead to the other.

While they were standing there, Ethan came up the steps from the dining room, saw Theadora... and stared. "What did you do?"

Smiling shyly, with her coat slung over her arm, she responded, "What do you think?"

His gaze traveled from her tooled boots, up the gray jeans that fit her slim legs as if they were custom-made. Her sky-blue sweatshirt with Crested Butte emblazoned across her breasts was baggy and unlike the feminine apparel she usually wore. But Ethan's eyes dwelled the longest on Theadora's hair. She'd had it styled into a swingy chin-length, easy-care cut.

"Well?" she asked a bit impatiently.

His expression grew perplexed. "What do you want me to say? You don't look like 'you.'"

Theadora smiled smugly. "I know. This is the new me, the Pine Hollow Lodge me."

His jaw set. "And what happens when you go back to Beverly Hills?"

"Maybe I'm thinking about not going back."

His frown was part confusion, part frustration. "Dorie, you don't belong here. You'd be bored in a month."

"Listen to me, Ethan Crawford. I've been bored the past three years... and lonely. Isn't it possible that your company and Pine Hollow is exactly what I need?"

The receptionist behind the desk had one ear tilted and was straining to hear every word. If Theadora didn't want to see her personal life in the tabloids, Abigail needed to interrupt. Touching Theadora's arm lightly, she suggested, "Why don't you and Ethan discuss this at his apartment?"

Theadora glanced around, realizing the girl at the desk had probably heard every word. "I don't know if there's any more to discuss. That depends on Ethan.''

He took off his hat and mowed his hand through his hair. ''I swear, I don't know what's gotten into you, Dorie. Of course, I want to talk to you. Come on upstairs with me while I make some calls. Then we'll have coffee or something.''

Theadora rolled her eyes toward heaven and sighed. ''Men.''

Abigail bit back a grin. The actress had made a monumental change in her life today, and Ethan didn't realize it yet. Or was he being purposefully slow on the uptake? Abigail put on her jacket and asked Ethan, ''Do you know if Brady's tied up right now?''

''Last I saw, he was headed toward his house at a fast clip. Luke's jalopy was parked in the driveway.''

Picking up her shopping bag, Abigail went to the door. ''Are you coming to the dining room for dinner tonight?'' she asked Theadora.

''No, she doesn't have to—'' Ethan started.

''Yes, I am,'' the actress answered at the same time as Ethan.

Abigail smiled and pushed open the door. ''I'll stop by your cabin around six.''

When she saw the snowmobile sitting zigzag on Brady's front yard, the side of its nose dented in, her heart raced and she jabbed his doorbell. Had Brady been in an accident? With Luke?

No sooner had she asked herself the questions when a blue pickup tore into Brady's driveway and skidded to a stop. A tall man with a ferocious scowl climbed out. Brady opened the door just as he reached the porch.

"Damn teenagers," the man grumbled. "Got no sense this side of the Rockies."

"Luke had an accident," Brady explained as he stepped aside for Abigail to enter.

Seeing Brady again, she remembered his good-night kiss after the sleigh ride and her fervent response. "Is he all right?"

"Thank God, yes."

"I don't know what's got into that boy lately," the man muttered.

Brady introduced Abigail to Will Underwood, Luke's father.

The man nodded to her, said, "Ma'am," then looked at Brady. "Where is he?"

"In the kitchen."

Will strode to the other room, mumbling, "I could wring his neck."

"Why isn't he thankful Luke's all right? And how about you?" Brady certainly looked as fit as ever. "Did you—"

"Luke took the snowmobile without my permission. He knows the combination on the shed lock because of the chores he does around here."

"Hasn't he driven one before?"

"Oh, yeah. His dad has one." Brady hesitated as if he debated with himself before continuing. Finally he sighed and said, "Luke was trying some stunts I did with it. I'd told him never to try it without train—"

A crash in the kitchen interrupted Brady, and he took off in that direction. When Abigail crossed the threshold behind him, she saw the can of chocolate powder, a spoon and a shattered mug on the floor as if Luke had flung his arms across the counter. He was standing with his fists balled.

"You clean up that mess," Will bit out.

"Not on your life!" Luke retorted.

"You want to be grounded two months instead of one?"

"I don't deserve to be grounded at all. Just because I had a little accident—"

"Little? You did at least three hundred dollars' worth damage. Who do you think's gonna pay?"

"If you let me quit school and get a full-time job, I could make enough money to go to Hollywood and get out of your hair."

"You need an education. I want you to go further than me," Will protested.

"I want to be a stuntman. I could be learnin', makin' some money, seein' places."

Luke's father shook his head. "I've tried to do the best for you. And all you wanna do is leave. If your mama was here—"

"But she's not. And you've got Sheila now. I want a life of my own," Luke said vehemently, his face flushed.

Will was immobile at least ten seconds. "Just because Sheila and me are gettin' married doesn't mean I don't need you, too. Don't you know that?"

Now it was Luke who became frozen. The stillness of the next few moments vibrated in the kitchen until the teenager's arms went limp, his face crumpled and he whispered, "Dad."

Tears filled Abigail's eyes as Will flung his arm around his son's shoulders. "Look, boy. I know you wanna see the world. And if you want it bad enough, you will. We'll yap about that when we get home. But right now we got Brady's sled to talk about."

Luke took a deep breath and said in a rush, "I'm sorry, Brady."

"I don't expect your dad to pay for this. I expect you to work it off. Understand?" Abigail suspected Brady's stern tone was more for show than from feeling.

"Yeah. I guess I won't be able to save any money for California until summer."

Brady nodded. "Probably not." He looked the boy over carefully. "Are you sure you're not hurting anywhere? I want the truth."

"My left arm's sore, but it'll be okay."

Brady said to Will, "Let me know if anything turns up. He'll probably be stiff tomorrow, but the snow's a good cushion."

"We'll let you know." Will gave a small smile to his son. "This kid's pretty tough."

Luke stooped to pick up the spoon, but Brady shooed him away. "I'll take care of that."

As Brady walked Will and Luke to the door, Abigail picked up the pieces of the shattered mug. Brady came back into the kitchen and warned, "Be careful you don't cut yourself."

He went to the closet, removing the dustpan and brush. "I know what you're thinking," he said.

She dumped the china into the trash can. "Yes, you probably do. Should you be encouraging Luke's interest in stunt work?"

"It's his ticket out of here."

She sent Brady a disapproving look. "You sound like Luke. *Education* is his ticket out."

Brady swept the chocolate powder onto the dust pan without meeting her gaze. "I agree he should finish high school. He can't go anywhere without a diploma. But Luke's never going to go to college. He doesn't have the patience for book learning. He needs something that's hands-on."

"Then he should try carpentry or...plumbing. Not something that can hurt him. I'm sure there are trade schools—"

Brady straightened and pinned her where she stood. "Would you be happy selling real estate or teaching math instead of doing what you're doing?"

His challenge and point were obvious. "Of course not. I found something I love—"

"So did I. And Luke has, too," he responded as he emptied the dustpan.

"Because of you," she reminded him. "Look what almost happened today. He could have been seriously hurt."

Brady hung the dustpan and brush on a hook inside the closet and closed the door with a none-too-subtle shove. "I'm not responsible for Luke's stupidity, carelessness and irresponsibility."

"No, you're not. But if he hadn't seen you do stunts..."

"Get real, Abigail. He watches stuntmen on TV, in the movies."

Why couldn't Brady see he was Luke's role model, his hero? "But you're here and now."

"Yes, and I'm trained, and I take precautions. Luke knows that, just as he knows I don't approve of what he did today."

They'd never agree on this point. Just the idea of someone putting themselves in a situation that could hurt them... What if Cole hadn't been a stuntman? She'd never say that to Brady.

"Cole is a different matter entirely."

Her gaze smacked into his, and she knew he'd read her mind. "Then why did you bring up his name?"

Brady rubbed the back of his neck as if the day's tension had settled there. "Because I knew you wouldn't. He could have crossed the street, gotten behind the wheel of a car, and the same thing could have happened."

"Then why do you feel guilty?" she asked softly.

He jammed his hands into his pockets and slanted her an angry glare. "Because I didn't prevent it. I couldn't stop his drinking, and I didn't catch him before he fell."

She didn't think before she spoke, and her estimation of the situation came tumbling out. "Only Cole could have stopped his own drinking. And the fall... You're not a superman, Brady, even though you might think you are."

"I don't think I'm anything of the sort," he muttered.

"Then stop beating yourself up for something you couldn't and you can't change. You're human, just like the rest of us."

Turning the tables on her and taking her by surprise, he asked, "Why so angry, Abigail?"

He'd read the feeling that had bubbled up inside her as she'd gotten to know him better. "Because you use this lodge, this life-style, as a shield to protect yourself from getting involved in life."

"I think you mean getting involved with you." His voice was low but pointed.

She felt a flush crawl up her neck. "With anyone."

Holding her gaze, he crossed his arms over his chest. "That's your opinion. The point is, Abigail, my life's my life and I'll live it as I see fit. No one else is going to tell me how.''

His angry determination shut her out. It was obvious he didn't want her opinion. She wasn't sure he even wanted her as anything more than a release for sexual frustration.

Tearing her gaze from his, she walked out of his kitchen. Then she kept walking right out his front door, unreasonably hurt, unreasonably angry and unreasonably falling in love.

''She thinks Luke's accident was my fault,'' Brady told his father angrily as he paced in front of his fireplace.

''From what I understand, Abigail's seen a bunch of accident victims. You can't blame her for not likin' the idea of anyone getting hurt.''

''Do you think it was my fault? Do you think I shouldn't be training him, showing him what I know?''

Ethan crossed his ankle over his knee. ''Do you know how long it's been since you asked my advice?''

Brady stopped pacing, saying softly and slowly, ''I can't remember the last time.'' When he'd decided to move out here, he'd asked his dad to be his partner; he hadn't asked his advice. When he'd told his dad about Solomen's offer to make the lodge into a camp for stuntmen, he'd just said he was considering a trip to L.A. to find out more about it. Again, he hadn't asked Ethan's advice.

His father stretched his arm along the back of the sofa, remembering the last time. ''You'd just met Carol. You knew she didn't like your work, and you wondered if you should get involved.''

"And you told me I shouldn't."

"That's because I could see something in Carol you couldn't."

Brady had always wondered what his dad had against Carol. "What?"

"She was the clinging vine type, the type that wraps herself around you and squeezes out your life."

"Dad..." Brady had tried not to hold on to any bitterness so he'd ended up with guilt.

"You know I'm right. Yes, you might have loved her. She was pretty and sweet and hung onto you as if you were a lifeline. That made you feel strong. But you never really respected her, did you?"

"Of course I respected her. I never would have done anything—"

Ethan dropped his arm from the back of the sofa and cut in. "I'm not talking about the way you treated her. You treated her like bone china. But as a person, did you respect her?"

Brady gazed into the fire. "She needed so damn much from me."

"That's what ended your marriage, son. Not your job, not losing the baby."

The flames licked at the logs, just as his memories licked at his peace of mind. "But if I'd have quit—"

"You couldn't keep giving and giving and never getting anything back. Just because Abigail doesn't like what you used to do or what you're teaching Luke, don't make the mistake of thinking she's like Carol, because she's not."

After a moment, Brady turned and faced his father. "No, she isn't, is she?" He smiled. "No one could ever accuse her of being a clinging vine. The lady speaks her mind and acts on her convictions."

Ethan returned Brady's smile with a lift of his brows. Then he got up from the couch. "I'm meeting Theadora and Abigail in the dining room for dinner. Join us?"

Brady shook his head. "I think I'd better let Abigail cool off."

"Or maybe you need time to think about her cooling off?"

"Maybe." Brady paused and shoved a hand into his pocket. "You never answered my question about Luke. Do you think his accident was my fault?"

Ethan shrugged. "What's important is what you think. I'm just glad you're not taking responsibility for it automatically. That's progress if you ask me." He plucked his coat from the back of the sofa. "Don't let Abigail cool off too long. A snowstorm's sweepin' in tonight. It'd be nice to cuddle up in front of the fire with someone while it's roarin' outside."

Brady let that pass. "We were supposed to go to Gunnison for supplies tomorrow."

"We'll just have to make do. We always do."

Brady suddenly realized he was tired of making do. He wanted more.

Abigail had been aware of the sound of the snow-blower more than once during the night. Through the windows she couldn't tell exactly how much snow had accumulated. As she walked down the path to the dining room, she realized at least a foot had fallen. The snow had stopped, but the sky was still gray.

As soon as she stepped into the dining room, she knew something was amiss. She saw only three wait-resses in the large room. Theadora sat at a table by herself while Ethan filled the buffet steamer with sausages and bacon. Usually within the time breakfast was served, tables filled and emptied sporadically. This morning most of the tables were filled with guests, some waiting for more food to be delivered to the buffet servers.

Abigail went to Theadora's table. "What's going on?"

Theadora was wearing jeans and another sweatshirt she'd purchased. "There was an accident out on the main road. A bad one. Most of the staff can't get through. Brady's making breakfast. Ethan's trying to be three places at once. He won't let me help."

"Brady's making breakfast for everyone?"

Theadora nodded and gestured toward the left. "Those guests haven't eaten yet. They're waiting for their tables to be cleared. Fortunately, everyone understands the situation and they're being patient."

Abigail unzipped her jacket and hung it on the coat rack. Then she came back to Theadora. "I'm going to clear those tables. Ethan can't tell me not to help."

Defiance lit Theadora's eyes as she stood. "I don't know why I'm letting him tell me. Maybe if I pitch in, he'll realize I'm serious about fitting in here. He thinks it's merely a notion I've gotten into my head and I'll get tired of it."

Abigail suspected Theadora had more spunk than Ethan gave her credit for. She and the actress plucked trays from a utility cart and collected used dishes and silverware. As soon as Ethan saw Theadora, he came toward her, his glare angry and warning. "I told you we don't need your help. Look at all the people watching you. They know who you are!"

"Fine. They know who I am. Are you going to turn down Abigail's help, too?" Theadora challenged.

The actress had put Ethan on a very hot spot. He swore. "Dorie..."

She piled dishes onto the tray as she talked. "I'm not some delicate flower that needs to be pampered, primped and protected. And if you're so proud you can't accept help when it's offered, then you're a fool." Picking up the tray, she faced him squarely. "If you can't accept my help, just pretend I'm doing this for Brady." She didn't wait for his response but took off for the kitchen.

Ethan swore again, glanced at Abigail and went to the buffet line to pick up the empty serving trays.

In the next hour, Abigail didn't get a chance to talk to Brady. Their gazes connected when she stopped in the kitchen to pick up a refilled coffeepot or to help him watch the sausages, or to take more food to the buffet line. She'd thought about their discussion yesterday, Brady's flare of temper, her exit. Tossing and turning throughout the night, the acknowledgment she was falling in love with him had become as real as the birthmark on her face. She could gloss it over, hide from it, but it wouldn't go away.

Even though she thought stunt work was crazy and dangerous, she had no right to judge Brady. At the first opportunity, she needed to tell him that.

Finally the dining room emptied. Theadora removed the apron she'd found somewhere and laid it over a chair back. Ethan pulled the white cloths from the tables. Theadora approached Abigail as she lined up salt-and-pepper shakers on the utility cart. "I'm going back to my cabin. Do you have plans for this afternoon?"

"No."

"If you get the chance, stop by. I need your opinion on what to wear tomorrow night for New Year's Eve. Ethan's taking me to a party at one of the hotels in Crested Butte. That is, if we're still speaking." She glanced at Ethan. His gaze met hers, but he turned away and yanked another cloth from a table.

"It's hard to believe it's New Year's Eve already," Abigail mused.

"I understand all the guests from Pine Hollow are invited. Are you going?"

Abigail had seen the notice in the lobby. "I don't know yet."

"Does it depend on Brady?" Theadora asked, her hazel eyes twinkling mischievously.

"Possibly," Abigail answered, anxious to apologize to Brady yet fearful further involvement could mean rejection.

After Theadora had gone, Abigail took a deep breath and pushed open the door to the kitchen. Brady was loading glasses into the dishwasher.

When she crossed to him, he looked up. "Thanks for your help. It's difficult to watch eggs, toast and sausage at the same time."

She'd turned the sausages on the grill while he'd scrambled the eggs. "I was glad to help. Considering how little you had, breakfast went smoothly."

"It's lunch I'm worried about. I'm not a chef, and our supplies are low. We've got plenty of chicken I can bake and baste with barbecue sauce for dinner if the road stays blocked, but lunch has me stumped."

"If you show me what you have, maybe I can help you think of something."

"Are you sure you don't have better things to do?"

There was still an awkwardness between them that was her fault. "If you don't want me here . . ."

He was quick to respond. "I didn't say that."

"I'm sorry," she blurted out, not knowing how to ease into their disagreement tactfully.

His thick brows drew together, his forehead creased. "For what? Speaking your mind?"

"For judging you. What you do is none of my business."

He took a few steps closer to her. "But you don't like what I do."

Her heart fluttered. Brady's physical presence always had an effect on her nervous system. "It doesn't matter what I like."

"Maybe it does," he said softly as he took a lock of her hair between his fingers and rolled it between his thumb and forefinger.

Every part of her felt alive and she almost felt dizzy with him standing so near. "I like you," she whispered.

His half smile tilted his lips. "Enough to spend New Year's Eve with me?"

She remembered the sign in the lobby. "In Crested Butte?"

He shook his head. "How about a late dinner at my house?"

Her mouth went dry as pictures played one after the other in her mind. Erotic pictures. "I don't know. I . . ."

He tucked the lock of hair behind her ear. "Abigail, nothing will happen that you don't want to happen. We can always watch TV and the ball falling on Times Square."

His reassurance wasn't necessary. She trusted him; she didn't know if she trusted herself. But having dinner with Brady, a quiet evening, would give her a chance to spend time with him, but more important, time to tell him about her face. "I'd like to spend New Year's Eve with you."

He stroked her cheek and dropped his hand. "Good." Turning on the dishwasher, he motioned toward the back of the kitchen. "Okay, Ms. Fox, put on your thinking cap. We're heading toward the pantry."

They decided to make ham-and-bean soup and tuna sandwiches for lunch. When Abigail saw the cans of peaches, flour and brown sugar, she suggested they make peach cobbler for dessert.

"Do you have a recipe?" Brady asked.

"It's one of my favorite deserts so I know it by heart. But I guess we'll have to multiply it by ten."

"You're the chef on this one. I can handle the soup."

Brady started the ham simmering while Abigail opened cans of peaches and drained them in a large strainer, then layered them in two giant baking pans. When she went to the pantry for the flour, Brady was already there, hefting the sack into his arm. "I'll pour for you."

The bowl was larger than any she'd ever used . . . or seen. Brady snipped open the twenty-five-pound bag and dumped it into the monster measuring cup Abigail positioned. She poured into the bowl and Brady refilled the container.

"Do you need the mixer?" He nodded toward the machine on the counter.

"I always mix it by hand. Let me try it that way first. I don't want the crumbs too fine."

Brady put eggs on the stove to boil for the tuna salad as Abigail stirred brown sugar into the flour. She found a pastry cutter hanging with the utensils, but when she added the butter to the bowl, she wondered if she could do it in one batch.

Brady was by her side before she finished the thought. "Need help?"

"Could you hold the bowl?"

He stepped close. Very close. Her hip bumped his as she picked up the pastry cutter. The flare of desire in his eyes seared her soul. Trying to concentrate on the dessert, she pushed the cutter into the butter.

Flour puffed up everywhere.

Abigail coughed. Brady jumped back. They looked at each other and laughed. Brady brushed flour from her chin; she reached up and passed her hand over his beard. She'd wanted to touch it freely ever since she'd met him. It was soft, not at all bristly. Running the back of her hand against it, she wondered what it would feel like against her skin, against her breasts....

When her gaze slid up to his, the deep green of his eyes took her breath away. There was hunger there, and desire, and need. He bent his head and she lifted her lips to his.

His arms went around her. Cupping her head, he kissed her with demand and the hunger she'd seen in his eyes. He didn't wait for her to open to him, but slid his tongue into her mouth with a possessive desire that had no time for coaxing or subtle persuasion. The thrust of his tongue aroused her until all she wanted to do was press into him, to feel more. He was hard where she was soft. He was strength where she was weakness. He was male; she was female. Together, they were dynamite.

As he assuaged the first burst of passion, he stroked her scalp. The kiss gentled and deepened. Sliding his hands out of her hair, he caressed her neck. His thumb measured her pulse right before he eased his hand under the neckline of her sweater.

She trembled and he kissed the corner of her mouth. Wanting his hand on her breast more than she wanted to breathe, she arched into him.

Brady covered her breast with his hand, gently kneading. With a movement as natural as the soft moan escaping her lips, she moved her leg between his thighs and pressed against him.

He sucked in a breath, breaking their kiss and his caress. "Damn it, Abigail, we keep this up and we'll have flour on more than our faces."

He was breathing raggedly and so was she. She didn't know what had gotten into her. "Brady, I didn't mean to—"

He took her face between his palms. "Didn't you? I did."

His gaze was so intense, she had to close her eyes.

"Abigail?"

Opening her eyes, she took a small step back. "We have to make the peach cobbler or it won't be ready for lunch."

"I suppose someone has to think about the lodge." His sexy half smile made her wonder if this New Year's Eve would be the most exciting she'd ever have, or the most heartbreaking.

Chapter Ten

The chef and another member of the kitchen staff finally arrived as Abigail and Brady took the peach cobbler out of the oven. Shortly after, Abigail left. She'd said she had calls to make. Brady suspected she was as thrown by that kiss as he was. Each one carried a greater potential for fulfillment. So did each touch. He ached just thinking about it.

When he went to the dining room, he saw his dad setting up for lunch. Two more of their staff came through the door. They waved as they shook off their boots and called, "The road's clear. Everyone should be in soon."

Brady took silverware from the cart and laid the place settings at the table next to the one his dad was setting up. "Looks like Theadora won't have to help clear tables for lunch."

"Harrumph."

"Did you say something?" Brady suppressed a smile.

"She's crazy. Did you see her running around here like a common—"

"Waitress," Brady filled in.

"I don't understand the woman."

"Wake up and smell the coffee, Dad."

Ethan's silverware clattered onto the table. "Just what's that supposed to mean?"

Brady kept his tone casual, not wanting to upset his father, but wanting to help him understand Theadora's feelings. "If you let her leave here, you might not see her again."

Ethan went still, then faced his son. "So what am I supposed to do?"

"Ask her to stay."

"She's got a mansion in Beverly Hills!"

Brady shrugged. "It seems that's not as attractive as staying here with you. She's sure dressing the part."

"I don't know what to do with her," Ethan muttered, shaking his head. "Where would I put her?"

"How about in your apartment?" Brady suggested easily.

His father scowled. "That's not funny, son. Theadora's a lady."

"Then ask her to marry you. She loves you. You love her. What's more important? The size of your bank account compared to hers or your happiness for the next twenty years? She retired because of you."

"Is all this advice because you asked me for my opinion yesterday? If so, I'm sorry I gave it."

"It's not advice. I'm just telling you what I see. And I see Theadora leaving and finding a new life for herself without you if you don't give her a good reason not to.''

Ethan turned his back on his son and picked up the napkins. One by one, he folded them meticulously, ending the conversation.

On New Year's eve, Abigail slipped on her boots. Because of the staff shortage the day before, she hadn't seen much of Brady after she'd left the kitchen. He had trails to groom, snow to blow and shovel. He'd stopped by her cabin last evening to confirm their date for tonight. They'd talked about everything from the history of Crested Butte and Gunnison to music they enjoyed. As they drank hot chocolate, the hours had flown. And when he kissed her good-night... She shivered just thinking about it.

It had been a casual interlude and again she'd thought about telling him about her birthmark, but, simply put, she hadn't wanted to. When she was a teenager, boys had turned away from her. They hadn't even bothered to get to know her because they couldn't get past her face. And when Stan had walked away from her...

She still remembered the pain. She was falling in love with Brady and she knew she had to tell him about her face, but she treasured each moment they spent together and didn't want to spoil any of them. She'd never considered herself a weak person. And maybe she wasn't weak.

She was scared.

Brady had insisted he'd come to her cabin and walk her to his house. When he knocked on her door, the warmth spreading through her could have heated her cabin for a week.

And as his appreciative gaze lingered on her turquoise two-piece sweater dress and traveled to the heels of her boots, the heat inside her could have warmed her cabin for a month. "Ready?" he asked.

She picked up her coat. "Yes."

Instead of setting the table, Brady had set two places on the coffee table in front of the roaring fire. Smells from the kitchen tantalized Abigail, but not as much as Brady himself. When he took off his jacket, she realized he wasn't wearing his usual sweater and jeans. His camel blazer topped a black silk shirt and black gabardine slacks. He looked sleek, masculine, powerful.

"Would you like a glass of wine now or with dinner?" he asked as he hung their coats in his closet.

"With dinner will be fine."

"It's ready. Have a seat."

"I can help."

He shook his head. "You helped enough yesterday."

Abigail sat on the sofa, her heart pounding.

Brady returned with two dishes. "I'll tell you right now, I cheated. I wasn't in the kitchen all day. This is beef burgundy from the dining room, though I did put the baked potatoes in the oven."

"It looks wonderful."

He smiled and so did she. They both knew what was on their plates couldn't have mattered less. "Save room for dessert," he warned. "I snitched a chocolate torte, too."

She laughed. "I hope you didn't take food out of someone's mouth."

"We always have plenty." He set their plates on the coffee table. "This seemed like a good idea, but we'll have to hold our plates to eat."

"Unless we sit on the floor at the coffee table."

His gaze swept over her skirt. "You don't mind?"

She grinned. "Not with a few pillows."

He moved the coffee table farther away from the sofa and plopped the throw pillows on the rug. "If you take your boots off, you'll be more comfortable."

She glanced at him. There was nothing suggestive about his suggestion. He nodded to the wineglasses. "I'll be right back."

Abigail sat on one of the cushions, her legs curled to the side. Brady brought in the wine, poured it, then took off his blazer, laying it over the back of the sofa.

As he folded himself down at the table, he asked, "Did you see Theadora before she and Dad left?"

"No. I haven't heard from her today. Were they speaking?"

Brady chuckled and shook his head. "Barely. Dad's been as grouchy as a grizzly."

"Who do you think will win?"

His full sleeve brushed her arm as he angled his long legs under the table. "I don't know. I'm just hoping he's not so stubborn that they both lose. They're made for each other."

"Your dad's old-fashioned. It's hard to put away preconceived notions about what men and women should bring to a relationship. I imagine he wants to feel like the provider."

"Theadora's smart enough to find a way around his objections. If he lets her try."

Brady's eyes met Abigail's and her heart turned over. He lifted his wineglass. She lifted hers. He clinked his glass gently against hers. "To a good new year."

"To a happy year." He searched her face and to evade his scrutiny, she took a sip.

"Music?" he asked, nodding toward a rack stereo system in the corner.

"Sure." He'd told her he was a Beatles fan and sixties music was his favorite. But that was not what came out of the stereo. It was soft and soothing piano and sax that added to the atmosphere of fire, wine and being shut away from the rest of the world.

They talked over dinner...about everything, it seemed. There was a lag in the conversation when Brady wiped a crumb from her lips and they stared into each other's eyes, searching, she wasn't sure for what. Her knee brushed his under the table and she left it where it was. He didn't move, either.

When they'd emptied their plates, Brady took them to the kitchen and came back with dessert. After settling in again, he smiled. "I forgot the forks." Instead of going to get them, he looked at her and said, "Then again, maybe we don't need them." Breaking off a piece of the layered chocolate, he held it to her lips. When she opened her mouth, his finger brushed her tongue. The desire in his eyes matched the fire burning inside her. She wanted this man. She wanted more than tonight.

She should tell him she was a virgin. She should tell him about her face.... Swallowing the chocolate, closing her eyes for a moment so she could think clearly, she finally said, "Brady, you should know—"

He leaned forward and brushed his thumb over her lips. "All I want to know is you. I want to kiss your lovely lips, touch you wherever you want to be touched and hold you close to me."

His words took her breath away. Yes, she wanted more than tonight. But if tonight was all she could have, she wasn't going to lose it. When he tilted his head and his lips covered hers, all her doubts, all her maybes, all her fears faded into wanting, and hunger, and a need so great nothing else mattered.

She was overwhelmed by Brady. There was so much tenderness in him, in his touch, in his kiss, but there was also a mighty passion that came from loneliness, and sadness, and pure physical power. As his tongue tempted hers to follow, to respond, to entice, her hands moved over the back of his silk shirt in the first eager caresses of discovery. He was hard, and taut, and hot. The silk was a tempting cover that only made her want to touch more.

When he dragged his lips from hers, she gave a moan of protest. Why was he stopping? Couldn't he see...?

"Abigail, I have to know you want this. I'm a lot bigger than you are. Tell me now if—"

She held his face between his hands. "I want you, too."

His sharp intake of breath told her that her words could excite him as much as his excited her. Pushing the coffee table out of the way, he laid her back on the cushion. His kiss this time was urgent, and demanding, and deep. She was swept up in the squall of desire.

His fingers fumbled on the buttons of her sweater. He started to undo them. Embarrassed by her inexperience, she tried to imagine what he'd like. She wanted to please him. Inhaling the musk of his skin and the scent of soap, she ran her hand down his chest, stopping at his waist.

He shuddered, and she felt his body tense. All his energy was going into control and restraint. "I'm afraid this is going to be over all too fast for both of us. It's been so long . . ."

Letting her love for him guide her, she reached for the buttons of his shirt. She'd already managed to unfasten them and found the damp heat of his chest, the springy curls of chest hair, when he sat her up and lifted her sweater over her head. He stared at the wispy white lace bra and closed his eyes for a moment. The expression on his face held pain and longing.

The same longing she felt to be close to him, touching him, pressed against him. With a boldness she'd never thought herself capable of, she whispered, "Take off your shirt. I want to feel my breasts against your chest."

He opened his eyes and swallowed hard. "Damn it, Abigail, do you know what you're doing to me?"

When she smiled shyly because she could only guess, he groaned and took a deep breath. After he shrugged out of his shirt, he reached around her to unfasten her bra. Listening to her intuition, rather than her lack of experience, she nibbled at his shoulder, smoothed her hands down his sides, glorying in his strength and virility. He shivered, and she realized how much he was restraining himself. She appreciated his chivalry, but it wasn't necessary. Loving was all about giving. She wanted to give him everything.

He pushed her back and stared at her face, the locks of hair curling on her collarbone, her breasts. The dusky rose peaks were taut, her nipples hard. Bracing himself on his forearms above her, he slowly brushed his chest against her breasts. She couldn't suppress her small cry. His chest hair teased her. His skin taunted her. And it wasn't nearly enough.

"Brady—"

When his lips surrounded her nipple, she cried out. The sensation was exquisite. His tongue was silky smooth, then flicking, then rough and sandy. She twisted, needing much more, wanting to pleasure him as he was pleasuring her. Mustering her courage, tamping down her insecurity, she slipped her hand between them and undid the button at his waist. As she unzippered his fly, he arched away from her. "Abigail, you can't. I won't be able to..."

His shuddering response led her. Giving was her only thought. She cupped him through his briefs, and she felt his arms quiver. His groan aroused her as much as his touch. Stroking him aroused her as much as his kiss. He had to know she loved him. He had to know....

He shuddered once, twice, three times, and groaned his release. Still braced on his arms, he went perfectly still, then lowered himself to his side.

She'd never imagined he'd be angry. But when she turned to look at him, he was.

"Why did you do that?" he growled. "Do you know how that makes me feel? Like I couldn't please you?"

Her heart almost stopped. "What makes you think you didn't please me? What makes you think that giving is any less wonderful for me than you?"

Rigid, his arms straight at his sides, he stared at the ceiling.

"Brady?"

He looked at her then, and his anger turned to amazement. Shaking his head, he said, "I've never met anyone like you."

She smiled. "Is that good or bad?"

With the sexy half smile she loved, he propped himself on his elbow. "Definitely good. Hard to get used to." Reaching toward her, he traced his forefinger across her lips, down her chin and the graceful sweep of her throat. He circled her breast. "But I'm trying. Real hard."

She trembled as the callused pad of his finger slid over her nipple.

Cupping the back of her head, he admitted, "I just have to change my thinking a little bit. Instead of believing everything's over, maybe I can realize it's just beginning. For both of us."

His lips were sensual on her skin. He slid off her skirt and half-slip without hurrying. Her panty hose were trickier, but Brady made each inch he revealed a discovery, new territory to kiss and touch and arouse. Even her feet. With the silk now removed, he caressed each toe, watching her eyes, watching the pleasure she found in his touch. She'd never realized her ankles were so sensitive, that his beard could make goose bumps break out all over from a simple brushing back and forth across her calf.

And her inner thighs...

"Like silk," he murmured, as he stroked and kissed and tongued until she was writhing on the rug. She reached for his head, her fingers kneading his scalp. The tension inside her was curling, curling, curling into a ball of need. He kissed her navel, tasted her hips and finally removed her panties.

"I want you naked, too," she murmured.

He grinned. "If you insist."

He was magnificent with his clothes on. She'd felt his powerful arousal when she'd stroked him. But without his clothes, Brady was imposing, daunting, more virile than she could comprehend. His muscles were so well-defined, a sculptor couldn't find a more perfect model.

But when she reached out to touch him, he backed away and said, "Uh-uh, lady. It's your turn."

Spreading her legs with gentle strength, he bent his head and kissed her so intimately, tears came to her eyes. Before she could brush them away, his tongue touched her most secret place, and her breath caught. The wild sensation left her panting. A spiraling excitement built until she grasped his shoulders, tossed her head from side to side and whispered his name.

He didn't lift his head but stroked and flicked and aroused until a wave crashed over her, then another, and another. She clutched at him when the climax hit, shocking her, shaking her, making her cry, "Brady!"

"I'm here, Abigail. And it's not over yet."

Still wanting him, still needing him, she reached out to him. She heard the quick tearing of foil, and then he was poised over her.

He slowly entered her, but when he met a barrier, he stopped. He asked hoarsely, "Are you a virgin?"

"I don't want to be anymore. I want you to make love to me."

"Abigail..."

"I want you, Brady."

Passion flared dark and hot in his eyes, though his entry was slow, restrained and oh, so tender. The slash of pain was momentary. With all the gentleness that was Brady, he stroked slowly. But she didn't want gentle and slow now, she wanted the fast, furious fulfillment only he could give her. Heeding ages-old instinct, gripping him with her thighs, she locked her arms around his neck. He thrust deep inside her and groaned.

Wrapping her legs around his hips, she drove him deeper still. His lips found hers and he ravished her mouth, plunging in his tongue, sweeping her with him to a place so extraordinary, she knew she'd never find it without Brady. He took her there slowly, then faster, then with a feverish pitch that had her arching into him to speed their journey so they could soar to the destination.

Her skin was slick against his, his kisses hot, wet and frenzied, until, with a surge that left them both gasping, he plunged into her and the snow-capped mountains met the clear blue beyond. White flashed, azure shot through it, a swirl of sunbeams burst all around her. She was one with Brady and love ruled the world.

The alarm was a distant ring. Abigail snuggled into the heat beside her, warm skin against her cheek, the brush of hair against her nose. But it moved away and she sighed with disappointment. The pillow beside her was a poor substitute for Brady.

"I'll be there in about fifteen minutes," she heard him say. Abigail opened her eyes. Brady put the phone back in its cradle, turned to her with a wry smile and kissed her forehead. "I have to go to the lodge. A problem with plumbing in one of the rooms."

"Ethan's not there?" she mumbled, pushing her hair from her eyes.

"They said they can't find him."

"What time is it?"

"Six-thirty."

"Are you worried?"

Brady shook his head, his mussed hair dipping over his brow. "Normally I would be. But since he and Theadora were together last night, maybe they stayed in Crested Butte. They probably decided after it was too late to call."

She put her hand to her cheek. "Brady, I have to talk to you about—"

"I have to talk to you, too. But right now I have to get over there." He kissed her quickly but soundly on the lips. "I don't know how long this will take. If you're not here when I get back, I'll come to your cabin." Swinging his legs over the bed, he reached for his jeans and flannel shirt on a nearby chair. "You go back to sleep if you can."

With a smile and a second quick kiss, he was gone. Minutes later she heard the front door shut.

Abigail looked at the empty place beside her on the bed. Brady's bed. He had carried her there after the most wonderful lovemaking she'd ever imagined. And then after they'd slept awhile, she'd awakened and they'd made love again.

She loved Brady. She had no doubts about that. And now after such a wonderful night, she was scared to death. Because she had to tell him about her face. It was the only honest thing to do.

Hopping off the bed, she looked in his mirror. Nothing showed, except maybe her love for Brady. She would prefer to tell him first, rather than show him. That way maybe his shock wouldn't be so great. She'd showed Stan. His response had been devastating. Or so she'd thought. But Brady's rejection would be even worse. She'd never felt like this about Stan.

Go back to sleep? No way. She would go down and clean up the remnants of supper, and then if Brady hadn't returned, she would go back to her cabin and wait.

Brady was filthy. He didn't know how the sink in room 220 had gotten stopped up so badly, but it had. Unplugging it had taken a lot longer then he planned. If Abigail was still at his house, maybe they could shower together. He smiled and felt a wonderful warmth he'd never felt before.

He descended the steps to the first floor, seeing Abigail as she'd looked naked before him last night. A virgin. He'd never suspected. She was so independent, so assertive. Why no man before him? There had to be a reason. A woman like Abigail was too special for any man to ignore. Last night he hadn't cared why. He'd just thanked his lucky stars, which hadn't been lucky in a very long time, that she'd chosen him.

But today he had questions. He wanted them answered. He also wanted her to fly to L.A. with him. Maybe they could take Luke and show him the world where he said he wanted to live.

If she wasn't where he'd left her, he'd go to her cabin. Another storm was moving in. They could light the fire, cuddle, talk. He hadn't felt this happy in years.

As he reached the lobby, he saw his dad coming up the stairs from the dining room, his dress overcoat hanging open over his suit. When Ethan saw his son, he looked sheepish. "Hi, there. Ned told me they had to call you about the sink."

"Yeah. They couldn't find you." He waited.

"I...uh...Theadora and I...we stayed the night in Crested Butte."

Brady said casually, "The roads were clear."

"Yeah, well, New Year's Eve and all. We figured it'd be best."

"One room or two?"

Ethan glanced around the lobby, but no one was there. "None of your damn business," he hissed.

Brady shrugged. "I guess that answers my question."

"I didn't say anything. And don't you go teasin' Dorie about it, either."

"Dad, calm down. It's all right. You two belong together."

Ethan took off his Stetson and rolled the brim through his fingers. "I'm gettin' used to the idea. I still don't like all that money she's got stuck away, and that big house...."

"You want her to give it all away?"

"Of course not. But I don't want a cent of it, and that has to be made clear if we're going to get hitched. We're still talkin' about it."

Brady clapped Ethan on the back. "Just be happy, Dad, and the details will take care of themselves."

"You look pretty chipper for having been gotten out of bed." When Brady shrugged nonchalantly, Ethan's eyes narrowed. "I suppose I'll hear about it when you're ready. But my guess is Abigail put that twinkle in your eye."

Brady shrugged again. "Could be."

"Texas is a long way from here."

"I know."

"Life's complicated, son. There's no gettin' around it." Ethan shook his head. "If you're goin' back to the house, I'll walk with you. Theadora says she needs some firewood so I want to get her some."

Brady glanced at the suit Ethan still wore from last night. "Like that?"

"Carryin' firewood isn't going to ruin it."

"Why don't you go on upstairs and change? I'll get her some on my way back."

"I'd appreciate that. I'll call her and tell her you're on your way."

Brady didn't have to knock at Theadora's door. She opened it with a smile on her face and a radiant glow about her. "Wonderful morning, isn't it?"

Carrying the wood inside, he laid it next to the fireplace. "Seems you and dad shared the same pot of coffee."

She chuckled. "Yes, we did." Sitting on the sofa, she crossed her legs and settled back against the cushions. "Can I ask you something?"

One of the logs rolled from the pile. Brady retrieved it and placed it in the fireplace on the grate. "Sure."

"I had a call a few days ago from my plastic surgeon. He wants to try again. I've talked to Ethan about this, but I'm not sure how he truly feels. I'm thinking about not having more surgery. How do you think he'll react if I have scars the rest of my life?"

Brady added two more logs to the grate. "What did he say?"

"He says it's my decision. But if we're together..."

Brady closed the fire screen. "Theadora, I don't know if Dad has admitted it yet, but he loves you. He has for years. If he says it's your decision, then he means it. I know he doesn't want to see you suffer anymore."

"And the scars?"

"I imagine a man in love sees beneath the scars or else doesn't see them at all."

"Abigail's so lucky that you won't care—"

Brady frowned. "What?"

Theadora suddenly looked nervous. "Uh...nothing. You care about Abigail, don't you?"

"Yes," he said slowly.

She looked past his shoulder rather than at him. "That's all. I think you're a fine man."

"Theadora..."

Her gaze met his, and she must have sensed more questions coming. "Don't push me on this, Brady. I've said enough. Too much."

He wasn't satisfied. He'd known Theadora long enough to know she was almost as direct as his father. She was hiding something. "Does Abigail think you should have surgery?"

"Oh, no," she said, obviously relieved to be talking about herself again. "And if I can be as happy with the makeup as..." Her voice trailed off and she cleared her throat.

"Theadora, what are you keeping from me?"

"Nothing." She stood and went to the kitchen.

"Theadora?" He remembered Abigail saying there was something she should tell him—on Christmas day and when they'd danced at Mountain Ridge. And just this morning again, she'd said they had to talk. He'd assumed she wanted to discuss last night, but...

"Is Abigail keeping something from me?"

The actress avoided his gaze as she took a bottle of juice from the refrigerator. "You and Abigail are none of my business."

"She *is* hiding something. What?"

Theodora shook her head.

"All right. I'll find out from her."

"Brady, don't be angry. I never meant—"

"I'm not angry. I'm uninformed. But not for long."

He left Theodora's cabin and headed for Abigail's. One lesson he'd learned in his marriage was that trust was everything. If Abigail couldn't trust him, how could they have a future?

Chapter Eleven

Laying her blow dryer on the vanity, Abigail ran a brush through her hair. Now that she'd turned off her hair dryer, she heard a knocking on her door. Hard knocking. It couldn't be Brady.... She stared at the jars of makeup on the sink. He couldn't see her like this. It would be too much of a shock. She had to prepare him first. She *had* locked the door, hadn't she? If she pretended she didn't hear—

"Abigail? Abigail, are you in there?"

She went to her bedroom and closed the door silently, then shouted into the living room, "Brady, I just got out of the shower. I'm not dressed." She heard his footsteps and her heart pounded.

"I've seen you undressed. Remember?"

Fear gripped her around her throat. She remembered Stan's face when she'd shown him her birthmark. The horror, the shock. She had to think clearly, she had to...

The doorknob to the bedroom turned. "I want to talk to you."

Her voice shaking, she dashed to the bathroom. "I'll be out in a minute. I have to—"

The door to the bedroom opened and she froze at the bathroom's threshold.

He didn't say anything. The shaking began with her hands and spread to her legs. Wrapping her arms around herself, she said, "I was going to tell you. I didn't know how. I tried...."

"But not very hard." His tone was cold and distant, his gaze staying on hers. It was obvious he couldn't bear to look at her face.

She felt tears surfacing and strove to keep them controlled. She would not let him see her cry. "I *knew* it would make a difference."

"What was last night about, Abigail? I thought it was about sharing, but most of all about trust. You trusted me to make love to you, but you didn't trust me enough to tell me about your face? What kind of a man do you think I am?"

"I was going to tell you last night, but then one thing led to another...."

"I'll say it did. You know what I think? I think you never intended to tell me at all. We'd have our fling while you were here and then you'd be gone. Why would I ever have to know, right?"

She flushed with guilt and couldn't deny that thought had run through her mind. But when she'd realized she'd fallen in love with Brady, she knew she had to tell him. "No. I intended to tell you. This afternoon. I was going to come back up to your house—"

"I'm supposed to believe that? You didn't tell me you were a virgin, either."

"Did it make a difference?"

"No."

"Does this?"

He frowned and asked curtly, "Your face? If you believe that, then you don't know me at all. What matters is your lack of trust. Relationships are built on trust, Abigail. I should know. I had one crumble because my wife didn't trust me. She didn't trust my love enough to know I'd never do anything to put myself in a situation I couldn't handle. She didn't trust that I truly loved her. Even when I quit the career I loved, it wasn't enough. Trust is either there or it's not."

Anger sprang up, replacing the fear. Abigail tightened the belt on her robe. "It's not that simple. I had a man walk out on me once before because of my face. I thought he loved me. I thought we'd have a future together. Then I showed him this." She indicated her cheek, her hand trembling. "And you know what he said?" She didn't wait for Brady's answer. "He said he'd never be able to make love to me if he looked at my face. I'd have to wear makeup. In other words, I could never really be myself. I knew, even with makeup on, whenever he looked at me, he'd remember, and nothing would be the same between us again. Because he'd always be wishing he was with a more perfect woman."

"He was a fool," Brady growled.

"No. He was representative of all the boys who wouldn't talk to me, let alone date me, before I found the makeup. He was representative of all the people who stare every time I go to the grocery store without it. He wasn't a fool. He simply didn't want a woman who was damaged. And believe me, Brady, in my profession, I see many men like that. They're not unusual."

"Abigail—"

"No. I don't want to hear it. You come barging in here thinking that trust is as easy as . . . as . . . making a snow angel. Well, it's not. It's more like leaping off the edge of the world." He reached for her, and she backed away. "Do me a favor, Brady. You think about it. You see me like this in your mind's eye. You imagine making love to me without my makeup. And when you're good and sure, then you come back and you tell me making love to me won't be different, that you don't wish I had a perfect face."

He stepped back, taking a long look at her rigid stance, her chin tilted high, the challenge that emanated from her with each breath. Then, with his expression giving away nothing, with his eyes shuttered, he turned and walked away.

It was what she'd told him to do. So why did she feel so empty, so cold and so alone?

The skis Abigail had used before sat in the storeroom. So did the boots. Taking them through the dining room, she wasn't surprised when one of the staff glanced at her once, then took a second look. He examined her face, then ducked his head as if he was embarrassed she'd caught him staring. Abigail sighed. It was always the same.

Pulling her wool hat on her head, she opened the door and went outside. Even knowing she wasn't supposed to ski alone, she just couldn't abide the thought of being with anyone right now. Her feelings were too raw. The gray sky looked threatening, but she could always turn back; there were trail markers all along the way. She'd be fine.

Pushing off, she knew she needed to work off her agitation and most of all her fear. Brady had said her face didn't matter. Yes, he'd said it. And that's what she'd wanted to hear. But did he mean it? If he did, could he forgive her deception?

She'd always heard that love made people do crazy things. She'd never believed it. If a person was honest, she was honest. That wouldn't change because she fell in love, would it? But loving opened many doors to possible hurt. The doors of rejection, abandonment, nonacceptance. Loving Brady had given him the power to hurt her. If she wasn't careful. If she let him.

Yes, she counseled her clients to be honest about their scars, to share their pain. Yet, when it was her heart involved, she couldn't do it. Now she'd still give the same advice, but maybe not so easily. It wasn't any easier to disclose than to trust.

Abigail attached her skis, hoping a brisk tour on the trail would calm her, ease her fears or exhaust her so she would stop thinking about Brady and whether or not they had a future.

She'd covered almost half the trail when the snow began falling, gently at first, then faster. But she kept going. It would be just as quick to take the shortcut Brady had shown her than to turn around and go back. The damp cold seeped through her even with the exertion. Soon it was hard to see twenty feet ahead. What had begun as a gentle snowfall was fast turning into a low-visibility blizzard. Wind swirled around her and she kept her eyes on the edges of the groomed trail.

Abigail didn't know how long she kept gliding one ski beside the other. But fatigue made the effort to push, see and fight the wind even more difficult. She thought she'd recognize the clump of trees where the shorter trail forked off. But she didn't; they all looked the same. That particular trail marker should have been obvious. It was red and four feet tall. Could she have already passed it?

Brady's warning echoed in her mind. *Don't ever ski alone.*

Now she knew why. You couldn't trust your own judgment. You couldn't trust your ability to remember. You could be too upset to care.

Brady trekked through the blowing snow, determined to set things right with Abigail. *He'd* been the fool. What Abigail had needed was acceptance, unconditional acceptance. But no, he'd let his failed marriage to Carol color his attitude. Abigail had made him think. But most of all she'd made him feel.

Maybe trust wasn't so easy. It had never been a problem for him. His mother had loved him and protected him until her death. And since then, his father had stood by him and never let him down. Maybe if he'd understood how difficult it was for Carol to trust, they'd still be together.

That was water under the bridge. He couldn't do anything about the past. But he could do something about his future.

He'd done what Abigail asked. He'd thought about seeing her day after day without her makeup. He'd thought about making love to her. And he'd gotten hot all over thinking about it. Her birthmark didn't matter, not to him. He ached for her, for the rejection she must have faced in her life. Finally he understood why she'd chosen this line of work, how she could help her clients so easily and reach them so well. She understood their emotions and their pain.

Brady knocked on Abigail's cabin door. He'd been stupid to barge in on her like that, not to let her come to him in her own time. And she would have. He knew that now. Too late.

She didn't answer, and when he tried the knob, he found the door locked. Pounding, he called her name. He saw no lights lit inside. Unless she was sleeping, that was unusual. Maybe she was with Theadora.

But when Theadora told him she hadn't seen Abigail, he began to worry. The snow was coating the countryside. Theadora tried to reassure him. "Maybe she's at the lodge. She's met a lot of people while she's been here."

"Theadora, I know about her birthmark. I barged in and saw it. She was upset. I was upset. I can't imagine her going over to the lodge to have afternoon tea with someone."

Theadora looked worried now. "Call me when you find her."

Brady assured her he would and went to the lodge. He asked everyone he saw if they'd seen Abigail. And finally when he talked to a waiter setting up the dinner tables and found out she'd left with skis, Brady's heart almost stopped. She couldn't be out in this storm; she just couldn't.

But she was. The skis she'd used before were missing and so were the boots. So was she.

Brady found his father and told Ethan that Abigail had gone skiing alone, and he was going after her in the snowmobile. Ethan looked as worried as Brady felt.

In the shed, Brady hung a whistle around his neck. He'd find her or die trying.

He searched the groomed trail. He knew it as well as he knew his name. Taking the shortcut first, he doubled back and drove the remainder of the long trail, with no sign of Abigail. *Frantic* wasn't a word he knew well or had used often. But panic and fear together caused frantic.

So, he started a methodical search, giving himself fifteen more minutes before he went back to his house and called for reinforcements. A search party.

When he reached the fork to the shortcut a second time, he blew his whistle long and hard. Then he blew again and again and again. Did he hear a faint cry? It could be the wind. It could be his imagination. He drove about thirty feet ahead and blew again.

Abigail thought she heard something so she yelled. She'd stopped near a tree to catch her breath, to ward off the cold, to pretend her limbs weren't getting numb from cold and fear and fatigue. She couldn't tell north from west, but the tips of the trees, their formation and positioning had looked familiar. If only she could get some sense of which direction to go.

She heard a sound again. A whistle? Harsh, shrill, too extended to be a natural noise. Cupping her hands around her mouth, she called out, "I'm here." Her words seemed to swirl in the wind and blow away from her. She didn't know how anyone could hear her, but she had to take the chance. She called the words again and again and again.

Suddenly she heard more than a whistle. A motor? An engine? A snowmobile? Brady?

If she skied away from the tree, she'd lose her anchor. If she didn't, would he find her? At first, she thought the sound of the snowmobile came from the left, then the right. In the wind, she couldn't tell. Her calling changed to yelling and Brady's name.

Miraculously, the machine appeared before her, its snow-frosted nose still dented, a huge man sitting on the seat. She tried to move toward him, but since she'd stopped, her muscles didn't want to cooperate. Her skis seemed as heavy as cement blocks. Managing to raise her arms, she flapped them together above her head and called out to him.

In seconds he was in front of her, his arms around her. She expected a scolding, she expected anger; she didn't expect him to hold her against him as if he'd never let her go. She buried her cold face against his neck.

His words whispered hot against her ear. "I've got to get you back." He loosened his embrace and took her face between his gloves. "You're safe now. I won't let anything happen to you."

Stooping, he unfastened her boots from her skis; then he scooped her up into his arms. He deposited her far back on the seat of the snowmobile, then gathered up her skis and poles, anchoring them between two tree branches. After he managed to slide between her and the handlebars, he grabbed her arms and pulled her tight against his back.

"Try to hold on. I'll have you back in a few minutes," he said against her cheek.

Zooming over the new snow, she pressed into his back as the forward motion bumped her against him over and over. She held on as tightly as she could, thinking nothing had ever felt so sturdy and so good. True to his word, it seemed like only a matter of seconds until he pulled up at his back door. He slid her back on the seat and climbed off. Not giving her a chance to move, he carried her into the kitchen.

She glanced at the hot tub enclosure at the back of the house. "If you dump me in the hot tub, I'll get warm." Her voice sounded cracked and hoarse.

He didn't stop in the living room but carried her up the stairs. "That would be too much of a shock. It's better if you warm up slowly."

Sitting her on the edge of his bed, he pulled off her cap and gloves and unzipped her jacket. As the warmth of the heated house seeped through her, a lethargy overtook her. She couldn't lift her arms or offer him much help. He examined her fingers, warmed them for a moment with his hands, then moved to her feet, where he removed her boots and socks. He manipulated her toes, then pressed her feet between his hands. She couldn't help but wonder if she'd ever be warm again.

Suddenly she started shivering and couldn't stop. Her teeth chattered and she tried to hold them together. Brady didn't hesitate to undress her. When he reached around her to unsnap her bra, their gazes met. He didn't flinch when he looked at her.

Slowly and gently he grazed his fingers over her birthmark and stopped next to her nose. "You have freckles," he murmured.

She tried to smile, but tears blinded her. In a flash, he laid her back and removed the rest of her clothes. Then he covered her with two blankets and a down quilt. Holding her arms at her sides, she still couldn't stop shivering.

Quickly Brady stripped off his clothes and climbed in beside her. When she would have snuggled into him, he said, "Turn your back to me. I can warm you better that way."

She did as he said, all too aware of their intimate spoonlike position. He was warm, and she could feel his body heat seeping slowly into her. With his arms wrapped around her, he nestled his chin in her neck.

After a few moments, he swore. "Honey, I have to call Dad. If I don't, he'll send out a search party for both of us." He kept her against him but reached for the phone.

As he spoke to Ethan, his chest rose and fell behind her. "I found her. Not far off the trail at the fork. I think she's all right. I'll watch her carefully. If there's any problem, I'll call the doctor. Tell Theadora not to worry. You, either. I'll call you in a few hours."

Both of Brady's arms were around her again. And if she weren't so cold and tired, she'd enjoy the press of him against her....

When Abigail awoke, the room was dark and the wind still howled outside. She was deliciously warm and still snuggled against Brady. Wiggling her toes, she discovered even her feet were warm.

Turning into Brady's chest, she felt his breath on her forehead as he murmured, "I thought you might sleep all night."

She leaned away. "Have you been here the whole time?"

"You needed the heat."

She couldn't tell from the tone of his voice what he was feeling. In the shadows, she couldn't see his eyes. "I see."

Moving away from her, he switched on the bedside light. "Do you?"

They were in bed, naked, and she didn't know if they should be. She squiggled a few inches across the huge bed. "Thank you for coming to find me." She self-consciously let her hair hang over her marked cheek.

"Don't do that, Abigail. Don't hide from me. I've seen your face. It doesn't matter."

The afternoon's stress caught up with her and tears again filled her eyes. "Are you sure?"

"I'm sure. And I'm sorry I reacted as I did before. You had reason not to trust me. If I'd been hurt like you have . . ."

She reached out and stroked his beard. "I'm sorry I didn't tell you. But when I started feeling so much for you, I was afraid."

"How much do you feel, Abigail?"

She was afraid to say the words, afraid he didn't feel the same way. So she dropped her hand and hedged. "Enough to wish I weren't going back to Texas in two weeks."

His green eyes grew dark and deep. "I don't want a long-distance relationship."

"I can't stay. Not out here. I need to be near a metropolitan center. Even Denver is four hours away."

"I don't have a solution, Abigail. Not yet. But I do know I want to spend every minute I can with you. Will you come with me to L.A. next week?"

"What?"

"I have to go to L.A. to talk to some men about turning the lodge into a training camp, at least listen to what they have to say. I don't want to leave you here. We could take Luke, show him the sights, let him see what he'd be getting himself into. I hate to see him take off for California or think he wants to without knowing what it's really like. When he sees how unglamorous stunt work is, he might change his mind. What do you say?"

"You're sure you want me along? You and Luke..."

He tipped up her chin with his index finger. "I definitely want you along. I'll have to share a room with Luke, but I'm sure we can find a few hours alone. We can fly in on Monday, come home Thursday."

"I'd like to go with you. But I need to ask you something. What do you feel, Brady?"

He didn't answer for a moment. "I feel changed. I think about you day and night, and I wonder what we could have."

It wasn't a declaration of love. But then she hadn't declared hers, either. Were they both too cautious for that? Or did they see too many roadblocks?

He reached out and stroked her hair away from her face. "Do you have a headache or dizziness? Is anything numb or tingling?"

"When you touch me, everything tingles." Her honesty lit a fire in his eyes and made her own desire burn stronger. He groaned. "Abigail..."

"Thanks to you, I'm fine. You probably saved my life."

A shadow passed across his face. "Don't make me into a hero, Abigail. I'm just a man. A man who at this moment does not have noble thoughts. After the ordeal you went through, you should rest, and all I can think about is making love to you."

"I already rested," she said softly, hoping he'd move toward her, hoping he'd kiss her, hoping all her doubts would fly away.

He must have sensed them. "You're still afraid, aren't you? Afraid that your birthmark makes a difference. You, better than anyone, should know beauty comes from a light inside." He placed his hand where her heart beat. "You have that light, Abigail. Will you share it with me?"

Tears misted her eyes. "It's yours, Brady."

There was no hesitancy or caution or holding back then. There was only mutual need, mutual desire and an aching so deep, only complete union could satisfy it. When he kissed her, she could feel her tears falling down her cheeks. He pulled away to treasure them, to taste them one by one, and to bless her face with more kisses that burned away her doubts, took away her fear and encouraged her to return his tenderness and passion. She kissed him back with a freedom she'd never felt. The deep, swirling kisses took her to a place she'd never been—a place where she was accepted for herself, unconditionally, a place so beautiful, so safe, so rare, she wanted to stay there forever.

Brady had more than kissing in mind and feeding the first flames of desire. The inferno inside him raged out of control. Desperation when he couldn't find Abigail, the fear of losing her to a snow squall, had broken through walls of isolation and self-protection. He no longer wanted to face life alone or work at keeping safe rather than happy. He wanted to let his love for Abigail light his way and forge his future. Because he did love her. How could he not? She was compassionate, and warm, and honest, and everything he needed in his life. But she had a life of her own. What did they have to do to find a life together?

His hands shook as they caressed Abigail's back and streamed through her hair. She made him strong, she made him weak, she made him crazy with wanting her. When she touched him, he grew harder and stronger in her grasp. It was amazing that she could hold him, surround him, and he didn't feel trapped. He felt freer than he'd ever felt before.

He kissed her again, deeply, with all the emotion he couldn't find in words. He broke away, only to come back to her again and again. When her hands skimmed his back and her nails raked his buttocks, he dragged his mouth from hers, kissing her neck, her throat, the pulse point that fluttered with the same hectic rhythm he felt pounding in his head.

"My breast, Brady. Can you touch . . . Oooh."

He took her nipple in his mouth, sucking and teasing until she moaned again and arched for more. Using his beard and lips and tongue to tantalize her, he held her waist with his large hands. His fingers almost met and he was reminded how delicate she was. Until she cried his name and reached for him.

"I need you, too, honey. But part of the fun is in getting there."

"Who can think of fun at a time like this?" she whispered.

He laughed and it felt so good. Everything he did with Abigail felt good...and right. This was more than pleasure, more than filling a need, more than finding satisfaction by physical release. This was real. Abigail was real. And he wanted to make the moment last.

"What do you want to think of?" he asked, hoping he knew her answer.

"You. Having you inside me. Holding you. Showing you how much..."

Her voice trailed off and he wished she'd finish her sentence.

Her voice trembled. "...how much I need you."

It was enough. "I need you, too, Abigail. When I'm with you I feel strong, and whole, and no longer empty. How do you do that?"

"I don't know. I only know...I love you, Brady."

She was the courageous one, she was the brave one, and he realized he had a ways to go before he could be as free. But he could show her. He tried to show her in his intense kiss, in each caress, in the way his body unabashedly strained toward hers.

Rising above her, he took her face between his hands and gazed into her eyes. "Watch me, Abigail. Watch me make love to you." It was as close as he could come to saying it...for now.

He protected her and suddenly wished he didn't have to. But he didn't stop to analyze it. He couldn't stop for anything. He touched her first to make sure she was ready. She was velvet and heat. Her murmured approval led him to position himself between her legs, to lower his body to hers, to enter her with a shuddering groan. Their gazes held each other as their bodies met.

He wanted days and nights with Abigail, hours to touch each other, and talk, and play. Somehow he tried to convey that, to communicate with his eyes as well as his body. Her blue gaze was filled with the shiny love she'd spoken of. He sank into her slowly, giving them both lingering pleasure.

She said his name with a husky catch that made his heart trip. She clasped his shoulders with a loving need that he felt, too. She tightened her silken thighs around his hips with innocent desire that took his breath away. When he slid in slightly deeper, she lovingly contracted around him, taking him to the edge of control. And she knew it. He could tell from the small smile that tipped up her lips.

He was gone. He thrust in a rhythm that made her arch into him. He thrust slowly enough that they could almost breathe in and taste the pleasure building between them, appreciate it and wish it could go on forever. He thrust into her, trying to become part of her, needing to be one with her, hoping light could truly burn away the shadows.

Quickening the pace, he saw her blue eyes widen, her lips sensually part, her breath become a pant of pleasure. As ray after ray of heat pierced him, fired him, brought a glow to Abigail's face and a moan from her lips, he drove in farther and faster until the sun burst and the universe unfurled. He would never forget today, this moment, this woman. Not in this lifetime and not in the next.

Chapter Twelve

Abigail had bought her dress on Rodeo Drive. She'd been terribly extravagant. But seeing the fire in Brady's eyes every time he looked at her, she knew it had been worth it. The peacock-blue, long-sleeved sequined sheath molded to her, and the thigh-high slit opened when she walked. She'd never felt like a siren before, but tonight with her high-heeled silver pumps, upswept hair and glistening shoulder-dusting earrings, she'd never felt more glamorous ... or excited.

Brady in a tuxedo was more handsome than she had ever imagined. He looked so at home at Pine Hollow with the sheepskin coat, snow, mountains, wide-open spaces. But here in L.A., dressed in elegant black and white, standing on the pillared porch of a house that looked more like a mansion than a family dwelling, he stood out, seemed even bigger and more powerful. She loved him. She wanted him. They hadn't been alone since they'd left Crested Butte two days ago.

Luke cleared his throat, looking distinctly uncomfortable in his dark suit. He'd slicked back his blond hair, and his smile was uncertain. In a short time he'd realized life away from Crested Butte was indeed a different world—from their plane ride to their stay at a posh hotel. Last evening, tired from a day of sightseeing, they'd ordered room service and played cards. Abigail had taken off her makeup when she'd changed into something comfortable. Luke's reaction had surprised her. He'd studied her for a good long moment and then asked her what had caused it. After she'd answered his questions and told him about the makeup, he seemed to forget about it the same way that Brady had, the same way her friends had.

But tonight she'd wanted to look her most glamorous. When Gus Solomen had invited them to this party at his home, Brady had consulted Abigail and decided it would be fun and an experience Luke would never forget. She probably wouldn't, either. She couldn't imagine ever forgetting anything she experienced with Brady.

A butler answered the door, and Brady took her arm as they walked inside. It was glitz at its finest from designer creations to Waterford crystal. The living room was more suited to receiving the queen of England than to welcoming a family for a night of watching television. A person might be comfortable on the Victorian furniture for about fifteen minutes. The mirrors on one wall reflected the polished sheen on the hardwood floor as well as the highbrow elegance of the guests.

"Wow!" Luke tried to stare at everything at once.

"I'll second that," Abigail agreed.

Brady shrugged. "It's all show. For the most part the people here are the same as people everywhere."

"But a hell of a lot richer," Luke muttered, then glanced at Abigail and blushed.

"Money just means you can buy more things, Luke. It can never buy you what's really important," Abigail said.

"What's that?"

"Good friends, family, someone to love," Brady answered, his gaze locked to hers.

She saw emotion there, but was it the love she felt?

A tall thin man with wire-rimmed spectacles came up to Brady. "I'm glad you could come."

"It's good to see you again." Brady introduced Abigail and Luke to Gus Solomen then looked around for Lou Feeney, the man who'd put the idea of the stunt training camp in motion. "Is Lou here?"

"No. He hates these things. I understand you'll be seeing him at the stunt camp tomorrow."

"That's right."

"Some of the guys you knew are training the young ones now. So try to get around and say hello. You could be in charge of them sooner than you think."

"This isn't settled, Gus. I don't know if I want to change Pine Hollow Lodge."

"Lou is ready with some pretty persuasive arguments. Listen to him, Brady. It's not too early for you to think about lining your coffer for retirement. This could do that. It would be a lot easier than running a dude ranch."

"Pine Hollow isn't a dude ranch."

"Maybe not. But it's a helluva lot of work. I saw you maintaining it, remember?" Someone called to Gus from the room beyond. "I have to mingle. I'll talk to you again after you see Lou. You have my number."

Abigail saw Brady frown as the man nodded to Abigail and Luke and walked away.

Luke said, "I'm gonna go check out that table with food. Okay?"

Brady didn't seem to hear the teenager. So Abigail said, "Sure. Go ahead. We'll be there in a minute." After Luke made a beeline for the food, she put her hand on Brady's shoulder. "It's a lot to think about."

Her voice broke his pensive stare. "Yes, it is. Especially now. If I turn it into a stunt camp, what happens to you and me?"

Her heart tripped. "I don't know. I don't know what we'll do even if you don't. Do you?"

After a pensive pause, he answered, "No. Because you can't stay."

"I can fly back and forth."

He frowned. "And how long would that last? Knowing you, you probably have a breakneck pace now. It would wear on you, it would wear on us."

They hadn't discussed the future. Since the day she'd gotten lost in the snow squall, whenever they could, they'd been too busy enjoying each other's company, discovering responses and reactions to touching and making love in between laughter and whispers and stories about their childhoods. Brady had held her and let her cry out some of her sadness at feeling like an outcast for so many years. She'd held him as he talked of his mother and how much he'd missed her while he was growing up. Stunt work hadn't seemed important then. But it did now. Especially if Pine Hollow became a camp for stuntmen.

As much as she hated the idea of a camp that taught men how to take risks, she knew Brady had to choose what was right for him. "You can't make this decision with me in mind. You gave it up once for a woman. That didn't work out. You can't do that again. This has to be your decision, Brady. You have to do what's best for you."

"Even if it means losing you?"

"You don't know that would happen."

"I don't know that it wouldn't."

He wanted her to reassure him, but she couldn't. Her love was too new, their future too unsettled. Each of them would have to make one decision at a time, hoping it was the right one.

When she didn't respond, Brady straightened his tie and said, "Let's go make sure Luke hasn't eaten everything on the table."

"Brady..."

"We'll talk about it more tomorrow after I've seen Lou. Let's just enjoy tonight."

They ate, they danced, they mingled. Brady saw a few people he'd known when he lived in L.A. Luke struck up a conversation with another teenager who was starring in a popular sitcom. The two young men went outside to look around.

"Do you think they'll be okay?" Abigail asked, worried about Luke in the midst of Hollywood glamour.

"Greg's straight, even with his meteoric rise to fame. From what I understand, he has a good reputation among the other kids and the adults he works with. Jack over there gave me the rundown when I got us champagne." He tapped her nose. "So stop worrying. How about another dance? I hear a slow one."

She gazed up at him. "I've missed your arms around me."

He groaned and dropped his arm across her shoulders. "It seems like forever since we've had time alone."

His husky voice made her mouth go dry, but she managed, "I know." When Brady took her in his arms, she nestled her head against his shoulder, wanting and needing much more.

They'd danced for a few minutes, engrossed in each other, when they bumped into a couple on the crowded dancing area. Brady mumbled, "Excuse me," then, when he looked around, he froze.

"Brady. Is that you? What are you doing here?"

Brady's arm dropped from around Abigail and he stared at the blond woman as if he'd seen a ghost. "Hello, Mary. I'm in town for a few days. How are you?"

"I'm fine. And so are the kids. If you have time, you ought to come see them. You wouldn't recognize them. I'm remarried now." She smiled up at the man with his arm still around her. "This is Tom Garfield. Brady Crawford." She said to her husband, "Brady was a friend of Cole's."

Other couples around them stared curiously. Mary said, "I think we're holding up traffic. Give me a call, Brady."

Brady just nodded, put his arm around Abigail, and resumed dancing.

Abigail didn't need an explanation to understand the rigidity in Brady's body, the tension in his hold on her. "That was Cole's wife?"

"Yes."

The word was like a gunshot, and she should have ducked but she didn't. "When was the last time you saw her?"

"Cole's funeral."

She leaned back in his arms. "Brady?"

He looked at her then and she could see the turmoil, the guilt, the memories that still had a hold on him.

"Does she blame you for Cole's death?"

His mouth tightened in a slash, and she was afraid he was going to tell her it was none of her business. But then he gave a quick shrug. "I don't know."

"You didn't talk about the accident?"

"No."

"Maybe it's time you did."

Anger flashed in his green eyes. "You think it's that easy?"

"I know it's not. But do you want to spend the rest of your life blaming yourself for something you couldn't prevent?"

The anger dissipated as quickly as it had erupted. "You think talking to Mary will change that?"

"It might help. What have you got to lose? She certainly doesn't seem hostile."

He looked over Abigail's shoulder. "No, she doesn't. At the funeral she was too upset to say much at all."

"She didn't turn you away, did she?"

"No. She's not that type of woman."

"You were friends with her as well as Cole?"

He brought his gaze back to hers. "Sure. Before I married, I had more meals at their house than I did at my own."

"Talk to her, Brady. Try to put some of the ghosts to rest."

He was remote for another second or so; then he pulled her closer, bringing her hand tight into his chest. "I don't usually take advice well."

She tipped her chin up. "Don't look at it as advice. Look at it as a suggestion."

He smiled then. "You're too smart."

She shook her head. "I love you, Brady. It has nothing to do with being smart. I care about your happiness." His gaze bored through her as he seemed to search her heart. It was open to him.

"What would make me happy would be to sneak away to one of the bedrooms upstairs and lock the door."

She laughed. "Think anybody would miss us?"

His brows rose. "You mean you're game?"

"You looked shocked, Mr. Crawford. Can't you believe I want to make love to you as much as you want to make love to me?"

"That's it," he muttered, as he circled her waist and guided her toward the stairs. "If I have to spend the night in a room with Luke, we deserve a few minutes to ourselves."

"A few minutes?"

"As long as it takes until we're both satisfied."

The husky promise in his voice made her examine again the distance between Houston and Crested

Butte. There had to be a way to bridge it. There had to be.

Anticipation built as they climbed a wide open staircase to the second floor. At the top of the steps, Brady's arm curled around her waist. Excitement escalated as he held her close, their hips bumping, his fingers scorching into her as they passed two rooms and turned left into another wing. Suddenly he stopped before one decorated in greens and navy, pulled her inside and closed the door.

With his one arm holding her close to him, his other snaked behind his back, and she heard the click of the lock. A thrilling shiver crept up her spine. She'd done few naughty things in her life. She'd never realized before how much fun it could be, let alone arousing.

Brady bent his head and kissed her with a hungry demand that gave her no chance to think. She could only feel—Brady's bottomless desire, her wild response, the excitement of the situation. She met his tongue with darting thrusts that matched the strength of his. Her hips sank against his, and he rocked against her, inflaming them both.

He caressed her back with firm hard strokes that brought her breasts against his chest. The sequined silk, his starched shirt, rubbed against her nipples, creating a tight tension in her belly that demanded to be released. When his palms kneaded her bottom in a rhythm in cadence with his thrusting tongue, she tried to wedge her hands between them to unbutton his shirt. But she couldn't. The studs wouldn't budge.

He broke the kiss and spread nibbling kisses down her neck. "Abigail, I need you now."

"I need you, too," she said, her breaths as ragged as his.

As he nibbled on her ear, he moved his fingers, bringing her skirt up her thighs. "What do you have on under here?"

"Not much."

He groaned. "Thank God."

The lined silk slid up her legs until he held it bunched around her waist. "Do you often wear a garter belt?" he asked in a raspy voice.

"Only since I shopped in L.A. hoping we'd have some time alone."

His mouth came back to hers, and he kissed her with the same feverish impatience that matched the movement of his hands as he unfastened the garters and slipped her panties down her legs. They fell to her feet. Lifting each spiked heel, she finally pushed them away.

Brady fumbled with the fastener on his trousers. He swore when it caught.

Abigail giggled. "Let me." In a moment she'd unfastened the trousers and let them fall. Brady shook them off and skimmed down his briefs.

Taking her in his arms again, he lifted her, and as her knees hugged his hips, he entered her, shuddering with the impact of their joining. "You are so exciting, Abigail, so sweet...."

She moaned and gripped him harder, contracting around him, loving him. He drove into her again and again until she buried her face in his neck and cried his name. He found fulfillment a few moments later.

As Abigail's heart raced against Brady's, she wondered how she could leave him, if helping others was more important than her own happiness. Deep inside she knew she needed Brady, but she needed her work, too. Could she have both?

Abigail had never seen anything like it.

Luke's eyes almost popped out of his head. He couldn't see enough or hear enough as they walked from Brady's rental car to the trailer office. The whole place made Abigail a little nervous. She saw ramps along a road, and cars parked in zigzag fashion alongside of them. She saw motorcycles housed in a double-car-size shed. She saw men with helmets and padded suits, and she didn't want to imagine what they were going to do in them.

Her reactions and Luke's were vastly different. When she glanced at Brady, she caught him watching her. She gave him a small smile, and he took her hand and squeezed it. "You're imagining the worst, Abigail. This is where men learn to do stunts safely."

A rotund man in a gray suit, white shirt and black-and-white-striped tie came out of the office, a cigar hanging out of the corner of his mouth. He held out his hand, and when Brady extended his, the suited man pumped it vigorously. "How're you doing? How's your pop?"

Brady grinned. "Dad's fine." He nodded to the stogie sticking out of the man's mouth. "Lou, haven't you gotten rid of them yet? Don't you know they're not good for you?"

"Yeah, yeah. You sound like my wife. I've cut down to two a day. One after lunch. One after supper. It's the best I can do. So don't you hassle me, too. Now, introduce me to your friends."

After introductions were made, Lou took them on a tour. A mild breeze ruffled Abigail's hair. The sixty degree weather was a contrast against Colorado's cold. Abigail's slacks and blazer felt comfortable.

Abigail was as fascinated as Luke by some of the sets. In jeans and a pullover, Brady looked right at home in the Western saloon, where the chairs were made of light balsa wood, and the mirror was toffee glass, a special material that shattered like glass but didn't cut. All he needed was a gun and holster. Activity bustled everywhere. She wondered what that would do to the peaceful atmosphere of Pine Hollow. It would never be the same.

Lou took them by a field where a monumental crane held a cage suspended in midair. It had to be dangling at least a hundred feet up. Luke asked, "What's that for?"

Lou answered. "Bungy jumping. Stuntmen were doing it long before it became a sport. Quite a thrill, right, Brady?"

Brady's eyes sparkled. "Almost as good as skydiving."

Lou clapped him on the back. "Want to go up?"

Brady's gaze found Abigail's. "No, I don't think so."

Lou looked him up and down. "Don't tell me you're not in shape."

"No, it's not that."

Abigail's heart thumped faster than she could count beats. But seeing the worshipful look in Luke's eyes, seeing the excitement banked in Brady's, she knew what she had to ask. "What would you do if I weren't here?"

He didn't hesitate. "I'd go up."

Her stomach jumped, and her pulse pounded at her temples. "Then do it."

"Yeah, Brady, come on. It'll be great. Jeez, I wish I could go up."

Brady's expression was pained as he asked Abigail, "You don't mind?"

She couldn't lie to him. "I didn't say that."

"It's not a risk for me, Abigail. I wish I could make you understand that."

"I'll never understand it. But I'm trying to accept it."

Brady stared up at the cage for a few moments. "Okay, Lou. Bring down the cage. Let's do it."

Abigail felt as if she'd been kicked in the stomach. She went cold under her blazer as Brady tipped up her chin and kissed her soundly. Then he gave her one of those half smiles she loved. "That's for luck."

In that kiss she'd felt his excitement and anticipation. She'd felt his need for her to accept everything about him, including this. But she didn't know if she could. Standing with Luke, she watched Brady and Lou go to the crane operator and have a brief conversation. The operator climbed behind the controls and brought the cage down. Abigail felt perspiration break out on her brow as two men helped Brady into a harness. As the cage rose again with Brady in it, she could taste her fear.

One of the men on the ground held a radio control and she assumed Brady had its mate. She couldn't see Brady clearly, but she could see him step to the edge of the cage. She'd never been so terrified in her life. And when he jumped, she couldn't control her cry of fear or the trembling that shook her body. He stepped into midair and bounced on the springing cord until she turned away. How could he do it? How could he want to defy safety and gravity for a thrill that only lasted a few seconds?

She presumed the crane lowered him to the ground. She didn't watch. She heard Luke's war whoop, his excitement as his questions toppled over each other. "What was it like? Do you get dizzy? Did you feel like you were gonna touch the ground? Man, don't you want to do it again?"

Abigail faced Luke and Brady. Brady took one look at her face, slung his arm around Luke's shoulders and said to Lou, "Why don't you take Luke over to Buddy? He's going up next. He'll tell you everything you want to know."

Lou guided the teenager toward the crane.

"You don't even look like you jumped from ten stories up!"

"Abigail—"

"Is this what you want in your life? You want to bring this to Pine Hollow?"

"I'm going to talk about it with Lou. What I want to know is will you still love me if I do? You talk about love. I want to know what that means."

Her logic warred with her emotions. "Oh, Brady. It's not as if we could have a normal life even if you do make Pine Hollow into a camp. I'll be back and forth...."

"Or you could stay. Your clients can come to you."

"Most clients don't have the money to travel. If I do that, it would be like an elite private practice. I want to reach everyone I can."

"So whether I keep it a lodge or not doesn't matter. Because you won't stay with me anyway."

"You asked what my love means, Brady. I'm trying to find out. But you haven't even said the words. I don't really know how you feel."

"I just asked you to stay at Pine Hollow with me."

"Stay with you? In another cabin? Live with you in your house? Be a mistress, a partner, a lover?"

He swung away from her and stared out over the camp. "You're making this complicated, Abigail."

"It *is* complicated."

"Maybe too complicated?"

She closed her eyes and tried to will her heart not to crack. "Yes."

After a long moment, he faced her. "I'd better round up Luke. Maybe you could take him over to the cafeteria and get him a snack while Lou and I talk."

Brady had removed himself from her. She wanted to talk about them, what options they had, what compromise they could make, but she could tell he wasn't in the mood to talk. Not with her. And she wondered if he'd ever hold her in his arms again.

Later that afternoon, Brady felt like a caged tiger as he paced his hotel room. Luke had gone down to the indoor pool to swim before supper. Supper. How could he sit across from Abigail, pretend everything was all right—

The phone rang, cutting into his thoughts. He snatched it up, hoping it was Abigail, yet not knowing what he would say if it was.

"Brady, it's Gus."

"I haven't made a decision. I need to talk to Dad."

"Lou told me. He also told me the idea didn't seem to excite you like he thought it would."

It had felt great to be back in the atmosphere of the stunt camp. He'd missed the camaraderie, the work, the sets. But the jump. It hadn't seemed as thrilling as it once had. In fact, making love with Abigail at the party had easily surpassed the thrill of jumping into space. Making love with Abigail . . .

"Brady?"

"Yeah. I'm here."

"If this doesn't work out, I have something else for you to think about."

Great, just what he needed. "What?"

"I'm starting production on *Spies and Thunder*. Lots of stunts and special effects. We're shooting it down near Chatsworth. How would you like to be my stunt director?"

"What does that mean exactly?"

"You'd help map it out. Plan everything for the best effect. Hire the stuntmen. Are you interested?"

"How long for shooting?"

"Figure at least three months. Six at the most. You know how these projects go. And, Brady, if this one works out, the word will get around if you want it to. If you want to get back in . . ."

Gus's voice trailed off and Brady knew this would be a chance to get back into the swing of the industry. In the same instant, he also realized L.A. was a metropolitan center, the kind of place where Abigail could find scores of people to help. Could this be the answer? Or would she still have a problem with his profession?

"How long do I have to decide? We're flying back to Gunnison tomorrow."

"Two weeks enough?"

"Yes. I'll call you."

When he hung up, Brady picked up the telephone book. There was something else he had to do before he talked to Abigail about their future, something he should have done years before.

Brady stood in front of the rancher and pushed the doorbell at the Garfields' front door. Dinner had been strained to say the least. Luke had gone on and on about everything they'd seen and done in the few short days in L.A., not seeming to notice the tension. Brady knew it hadn't been the best time to ask Abigail for a favor, yet he'd done it anyway. He'd asked her to take Luke sightseeing for a couple of hours while he ran an errand. She'd only hesitated a moment, then agreed.

Mary Garfield opened the door, her expression relaxed. "Come in."

"I hope I didn't interfere with your plans."

"Not at all. Tom took the kids for new sneakers."

"Are you still working at the law firm?"

"Sure am. But I'm thinking about going to law school instead of being a paralegal all my life. The kids are old enough now. Ginger will be going to college next year, the two boys are in high school."

She led him into a living room with a cathedral ceiling. The contemporary striped furniture looked comfortable, but he didn't feel comfortable. He noticed a framed photograph of Cole with the children at the beach. Crossing to the television, he picked it up.

"Your husband doesn't mind?"

"He's helped me keep Cole's memory alive. I don't want the kids to forget him, although they do accept Tom as their father now."

"He must be a special man."

"He is. Not at all like Cole. Life with Cole was never easy."

Brady studied Cole's picture. "You never told me there were problems."

"But you knew, didn't you?"

"I knew Cole was troubled."

Mary brushed her blond hair away from her face as she shook her head. "He was always a little boy, Brady. He never grew up. When the kids came so fast, he couldn't handle the responsibility. That's why his drinking got worse there at the end."

"I should have done something. I should have gotten him help."

"And you think Cole would have taken advantage of it? Don't kid yourself, Brady. More times than you could count, I tried to drag him to the marriage counselor. But he'd find an excuse. Work would get in the way. He simply wouldn't show up. He wouldn't take responsibility for himself. How could we help him?"

Brady walked to the sofa, photograph in hand. Sinking down on the couch, he looked up at Mary. "We never talked about the accident."

"What was there to say?" He stared at her and planned to put his thoughts into words, when she sat down on the chair across from him. "What is it, Brady? What's wrong?"

"I felt responsible. I still do. And I thought maybe, all these years, that you might have thought I could have prevented his death."

She gasped. "I never thought that. Brady, you two were like brothers. Of course you would have done something if you could. I never had any doubt of that. Why do you?"

"I'm not sure. Maybe because of what was going on with Carol at the time, the responsibility I felt for her and the baby. Cole and I *were* like brothers, Mary. Maybe I wondered why it happened to Cole and not me."

She rested her hands on her knees. "You were never careless. You took your job seriously. Cole played at it. He was good, but I think part of him was self-destructive. You've got to let go of him, Brady. I have. Don't you think I felt guilty for all the fights, the arguing, the times when I should have been more understanding and I wasn't? But Tom helped me see guilt was useless."

Abigail had said almost the same thing. Brady set the photograph on the coffee table.

After his visit with Mary, Brady returned to the hotel but didn't go inside. From the parking garage, he took the elevator to ground level and walked up the street, hardly noticing the palms or the breeze ruffling his hair.

Even after all these years, the day of Cole's accident was vivid in his mind. The vibration of the train under his feet, the rush of wind, Cole just out of reach... Brady squeezed his eyes closed and took a deep breath. *Analyze it, Crawford.*

As if he hadn't a million times.

The point was he couldn't analyze what happened that day. He wasn't some objective onlooker like a director who could see the whole picture before he shot the close-up. Brady had been in the midst of it, lived the eternal moment when Cole had gone over the side, lived through the grief of losing a baby and finally losing his wife. Yet he tried to push himself back. He tried to look at Cole's accident, Carol's miscarriage, his years at Crested Butte as a self-imposed hermit.

Cole had chosen the road to self-destruction despite Brady's friendship, despite Brady's offers of help. Mary had faced her guilt. Now Brady examined his. He felt responsible because he cared, because he loved Cole, because he'd never wanted to believe he was powerless to help someone he loved. But being powerless in a situation wasn't a sin; it was sometimes a condition of being human.

No one could control everyone, everything. And sometimes love *wasn't* enough. Friendship—a relationship—required two people working together, not pulling apart. He and Carol had pulled in separate directions from the beginning of their marriage.

Brady's choices had led him into stunt work, to marry Carol, eventually to live in Crested Butte. But he also had to admit he couldn't control fate or other people. He could only control what he chose to do next. What mattered now were the decisions he made today. Maybe letting go of the past had to begin with the conscious decision of looking to the future. If so, it was time he made the decision. It was time he thought about a fulfilling life . . . with Abigail.

When Brady returned to his hotel room, he found Luke settled on the bed watching television. He told the teenager that he was going to talk to Abigail for a while. Luke just nodded, unconcerned.

Brady knocked on Abigail's door, feeling free, feeling relieved of a burden he'd carried too long.

Abigail answered the door, dressed in the blue sweat suit she'd worn the first day he'd brought her home from cross-country skiing.

"Can we talk?"

She gave him a tentative smile. "Sure."

Remembering the party, their frenzied lovemaking, he wanted nothing more than to take her in his arms. But he couldn't. Not yet.

Abigail went to the window and sat in one of the chairs at the small table. She looked as nervous as he suddenly felt. Sitting across from her, he crossed his arms on the table in front of him. "I saw Mary. We had a long talk. You were right. It did a lot of good. Cole had problems I couldn't solve. I realize that now. And the accident... It was just that. I had Cole and Carol caught up in my mind together, I guess. It's time to get on with my life."

Her voice quivered slightly as she asked, "How are you going to do that?"

"That depends on you."

"You're going to make the lodge into a stunt camp?"

"No. I called Dad before I went to Mary's. We like Pine Hollow the way it is. But I *will* still be involved in the stunt business. Gus offered me the position of stunt director on his next movie. It sounds challenging, it sounds like something I'd like to try. I'll be living near L.A. and this work could lead to more like it. You could move your practice here. What do you think?"

Chapter Thirteen

When Abigail didn't respond immediately, Brady went on. "I'm asking you to put yourself on the line. Either our future means something to you or it doesn't. On-again, off-again isn't what I want. But you have to decide if you're willing to take this risk, and to accept the business I'm in. The stunt business." He watched the emotions play across her face, heightening her color. He'd just noticed she wasn't wearing her makeup. It was funny how love and life-changing decisions put the world in perspective.

"I don't know what to say."

He knew he was asking a lot. But Carol's love had trapped him. It had been claustrophobic and limiting. He didn't think Abigail's was the same. With her he hoped there was room for exploration, for excitement and for change. Was he hoping for too much?

"I've thrown a lot at you and I know you need some time. Because you have to be sure, Abigail."

She looked down at her hands, folded in her lap. "How much will you be involved in the stunt work itself?"

"I'll be working with trained stuntmen. So I won't be doing stunts, as such. But I'm not going to say I never will."

"This is a test, isn't it?" she asked with a quick angry look.

"You can look at it that way if you want. But it's no test. It's a way we can be together."

Her chin lifted. "But I have to uproot my practice, move away from friends, accept the dangerous work you want to direct others to do—I have to do all the changing."

"For now. Maybe later it will be my turn."

Her angry silence told him she wasn't ready to give him an answer. It told him she wasn't sure about what they had. He pushed back his chair and stood. "Our flight leaves at 10:00 a.m. We'd better leave here about 8:30."

She stood, too. He saw confusion replace the anger in her beautiful blue eyes, and he knew he'd never wanted her so much. But they had to settle this first, if they could settle it at all.

She walked him to the door. He wanted to take her in his arms; he wanted to tell her they could work anything out. But he wasn't sure that was so. So he said good-night. With his heart aching because he didn't know if they'd ever be close again, he closed the door behind him.

* * *

Abigail hurried to Theadora's cabin. She couldn't stand being alone with her own thoughts anymore. The trip back to Crested Butte had been tense. Brady had brought her luggage to her cabin, looked as if he wanted to say something, but left without doing it. She hadn't seen him the rest of the day, or yesterday, either.

She'd paced, she'd cried, she'd stared into the fire, seeing them together skiing, cooking, making love. She couldn't stand the turmoil anymore. She had to talk it out with someone. Theadora was the logical choice.

Abigail knocked. No one answered. She turned away, ready to search the lodge for the actress if she had to, when the door opened. Theadora's eyes were bright, her hair mussed. "Abigail! Come in. Where have you been hiding yourself?"

When Theadora stepped back, Ethan appeared beside her. "I hope you're in a better mood than my son. He's been downright grumpy since he got back." Ethan curved his arm possessively around Theadora's waist.

"I didn't mean to interrupt anything," Abigail said, looking at the couple who'd obviously been enjoying some time to themselves. "I can come back later...."

"Nonsense," Theadora responded, taking Abigail's arm. "I want to hear about your trip. Ethan was just leaving."

His brows hiked up and he grinned. "Yep, I guess I was. But are you going to tell her our news before I do?"

Abigail stepped into the cabin and couldn't help but notice the radiant expression on Theadora's face. The actress smiled and said, "I'm moving out here with Ethan. And when he discovers I'm indispensable, he'll marry me. He needs someone to help him run this place with Brady leaving. I've got organizational skills this man never imagined."

"She's got more than organizational skills," Ethan muttered, though Abigail could see he wasn't unhappy about Theadora's plans for them.

Theadora ignored his grumbling. "We'll be cramped in Ethan's apartment until we can build our own place, but I don't think either of us will mind."

"I think the woman's dad-blasted crazy. She's giving up a house in Beverly Hills as big as the lodge to share an apartment."

"Empty rooms get lonely. Bumping into you in the kitchen is a lot more fun."

"Or in other rooms," he added suggestively.

The actress batted his arm. "Go on. I'm sure you have things to do. Abigail and I need to have some girl talk."

The obvious affection and love between these two brought tears to Abigail's eyes. Her throat tightened, and there was nothing she could say.

Ethan studied her for a moment, but Theadora took his arm and walked him to the door. With a quick kiss on his cheek, she said, "I'll see you at dinner."

He looked over her shoulder at Abigail again, nodded and left.

Theadora put her arm around Abigail's shoulders and guided her to the sofa. "Tell me what's wrong. I know Brady's moving to L.A. What are you going to do?''

Abigail sank down on the sofa. "He asked me to go with him."

"And?"

"I'd have to move my practice."

"Is that possible?"

"Anything's possible."

"What aren't you telling me?"

"It's the stunt work. He'll still be involved with it." Abigail told Theadora about the day at the camp, Brady's plunge into midair, her fear and panic as she'd watched. "I didn't think I was like Carol. I thought I was being noble, not wanting him to be involved in something that could hurt someone. But maybe the bottom line is that I'm worried about him."

"It's probably a lot of both."

"Theadora, I don't know what to do. I love him. But he hasn't said he loves me—"

"Ah-ha. So is it really the stunt work or the move?"

"I need him to tell me," she murmured. "I need to be sure."

Theadora shook her head. "You think the words will make you sure? I don't think so. Brady's a lot like his father. His feelings run deep, and he can't always put them into words. But what I've learned over the years is to watch what a man does, not what he says. I don't think Brady is moving to L.A. simply because he wants to get back into the business. I think he sees it as a way you can stay together."

Abigail's thoughts had been so chaotic that she'd never thought of that. "You really think so?"

"You think about it, Abigail. And you think about my life. I gave years to my career. But I was never really happy. I needed Ethan in my life. Thank God, fate brought us together now and we didn't lose our chance. Don't take the risk of losing yours."

Abigail took a walk to Pine Hollow after she'd talked to Theadora. She stood listening to the silence, the straining of snow-heavy boughs. She'd poured all of her energy into her work for years. Before Stan, because she wanted to help as many people as was humanly possible. After Stan, because she'd mistakenly believed no man could love her without her makeup.

No, Brady hadn't said the words. But hadn't he shown her by his acceptance, his kisses, his touch, that she was precious and cherished? She loved Brady more than she'd ever thought she could love anyone. Maybe that's what had scared her, too. Stan's rejection had taught her not to trust. But if she didn't trust, she couldn't really love.

What did Brady think now? That she'd said the words only to have them carry no weight when decisions and compromise were needed? What kind of love was that? Not the kind of love that could take them through a lifetime together.

Did he feel she'd rejected him? Did he still want her? Or had her uncertainty driven an insurmountable wedge between them? There was only one way to find out.

As Abigail followed the snowmobile trail into Brady's backyard, she heard the thud of the ax. Unintelligible voices floated toward her. She followed them to the splitting stump by the shed.

She approached, seeing Luke stacking the logs as Brady split them. The teenager was saying, "I promised Dad I'd graduate first. He said if I try to get decent grades next year, really work at it, he'll stake me."

"You can't ask for better than that."

"Sheila said she'll miss me if I go to California. Can you imagine? Do you think she will?"

"I think she cares about you, Luke."

"I guess so. But, man, I still want to get to L.A. Maybe I can live with you when I come out. I mean . . . just until I'd find a place and everything."

"We'll see. That's over a year away. A lot can happen. You might change your mind. I might be somewhere else."

"You really think I can do it?"

Abigail chose that moment to make her presence known. "You can do anything you put your mind to, Luke."

Brady swung around, his eyes shuttered when they met hers. He didn't look particularly glad to see her, and she suspected this was going to be uphill the whole way. But that didn't matter. Somehow she'd convince him that she loved him and was willing to forge a future with him.

"Hi, Abigail." Luke stacked the last three logs on the pile, paying no notice to her lack of makeup. "I've got to get going. Sheila's makin' an early dinner. I'll see you guys tomorrow."

After Luke had trekked around the side of the house, Brady stooped, picking up an armful of logs.

"Can I come in for a few minutes?" Abigail asked, wishing Brady would say something.

"If you'd like." His words were as cold as the air stinging her nose.

She followed him in the back door, careful to knock the snow from her boots. Not stopping in the kitchen, Brady went straight to the living room, dumping the wood by the fireplace. He didn't ask her to sit down, but she unzipped her jacket anyway. He'd have to bodily throw her out if he wanted to get rid of her.

He faced her, then took off his gloves and hat, throwing them to the coffee table. "When are you leaving?"

"Tuesday, but—"

"I don't need any explanations, Abigail."

That's what *he* thought. "I have a lot to do in Houston. Notify the doctors at the hospital I'll be moving my practice to L.A., try to get my office packed up, check my client list for..."

He looked shell-shocked. "Did I hear you correctly?"

She plunged ahead, praying she heard a hopeful note in his voice. "I want a future with you, Brady. I'm sorry it took so long for me to sort through this, but if you still want me, I want to spend my life with you."

The shadows left his eyes and his lips turned up in a smile. "If I still want you... ? Come here, lady."

She stepped into his arms and lifted her mouth to his for his kiss. It was hard and sweeping and told her the past few days had been as tough for him as they had for her. It created in her an aching need only Brady could fill.

He lifted her into his arms and without breaking the kiss carried her to the sofa, cuddling her in his lap.

When he finally pulled away, he tilted his forehead against hers. "I'd convinced myself it was too much to ask. I tried to convince myself I could build a new life without you."

"You don't have to. We'll build a life together."

He held her face between his palms and traced the edge of her birthmark along her cheek. "I love you, Abigail. Over the past few days I wished I'd said it because it might have made a difference. But I was afraid to, afraid love didn't mean the same thing to you that it meant to me. Will you marry me? Will you take a risk and go on a lifelong adventure with me?"

"Marrying you won't be a risk, Brady. I've never been more sure of anything in my life."

"That's a yes?"

She threaded her fingers in his hair and urged his head toward hers. When she kissed him, she nibbled his lips, slowly slid her tongue along their seam and then let him take over so he knew she was willing to give and take, to share, to trust him to love her his way.

He finally dragged his mouth from hers and took a deep breath. "That was a definite yes. How am I going to let you fly off to Houston?"

She stroked his beard. "If I postpone leaving, could you get away again to go with me?"

He kissed her palm. "I'll talk to Dad. Maybe we can interview for an assistant manager. He'll need one when I leave." Brady lovingly pushed Abigail's hair behind her ear. "Do you think we could talk about the details later? Right now, there's something else I'd much rather do."

She smiled and anticipation fluttered in her stomach. "Which is?"

"Make slow sweet love to my intended bride."

Locking her arms around his neck, she breathed in his scent, lovingly scanned his face and said, "I'd like nothing better."

Brady enclosed her in his arms and held her close to his heart.

Epilogue

Three years later

On a sunny June afternoon, Abigail stood in the
shade of the trees in Pine Hollow, holding her three-
month-old daughter in her arms. She lovingly adjusted Juliet's cap and straightened the collar of the
sweater under her baby's neck. "Listen to the birds,
sweetheart. And the whispering branches. They have
secrets to tell."

Her daughter wriggled and smiled at her.

Brady's baritone interrupted her interlude with their
child. "She can probably hear them better than we
can."

Her husband stood in the light of the clearing, the
sun bright on his head. He no longer wore a beard.
He'd shaved it off the night before their wedding,

telling her he wanted her to make sure she knew what she was getting. His lean cheeks, his strong jawline, only added to his rugged appeal. She loved him and wanted him more now than when they were married three years ago, here in this very place.

He walked over to her. "Theadora said the scavenger hunt at the lodge will begin in fifteen minutes. She'll be disappointed if her granddaughter isn't there to watch."

"She's made wonderful changes at the lodge. Whoever thought you'd have so many families staying in the new cabins!"

"I know. They actually talk to each other, and the kids play games with their parents instead of watching television."

"I haven't had a chance to ask Theadora if she regrets selling her Beverly Hills house."

"I talked to her for a while last night while you were rocking Juliet to sleep. What she regrets is that Dad won't touch any of the money. Marriage certainly didn't lessen his stubbornness on that issue."

Theadora and Ethan had married a few months after she and Brady. "I couldn't believe she set up a trust fund for Juliet. Should we accept it?" asked Abigail.

"I don't think we have any choice. We'll hurt her if we don't."

"Did you know she bought your dad a new truck? It's being delivered tomorrow."

Brady grinned. "Uh-oh. Could be trouble."

Juliet gurgled and Abigail tenderly brushed her cheek. "Theadora seems to have the bases covered. She said if he won't accept it, she won't plan the menus anymore and he'll have to deal with their temperamental chef himself."

Brady laughed out loud, a deep rich sound that echoed in the clearing. Juliet's gaze went to his face and she waved her arms. He held out his. "Want me to take her?"

"Sure."

Juliet nestled in her dad's arms, her adoring gaze on his face. Brady put his other arm around Abigail's shoulders. "Do you think we deserve to be this happy?"

Abigail didn't hesitate. "Yes." While Brady had worked his way back into the movie industry, he'd gotten more and more interested in special effects. When he worked on movies now for a special-effects company, he usually did so in the environs of the studio, where filmmakers tried to make the impossible look real. He'd found his niche, just as Luke had found his. He'd become an integral part of their lives, sharing meals with them often, taking Brady's advice about his stunt work. And Abigail had come to respect the craft as she would any other, recognizing her fears but seeing beyond them.

Instead of handling her practice herself, she'd trained makeup cosmetologists to help with her work. Not only had this change enabled her to keep her practice flourishing, but it had given her more time with Brady and now with Juliet. She and Brady came back to Pine Hollow Lodge whenever they could to see Ethan and Theadora, to take time for themselves. Abigail had never been happier.

And Brady? There were no more shadows in his eyes.

He pulled her close to him now, kissing her cheek, nuzzling her neck.

"Brady. Our daughter's watching."

"Good. She'll see how a man should treat the woman in his life."

Abigail couldn't keep her mouth from meeting his, couldn't keep the passion from igniting as soon as her lips touched his.

Brady ended the kiss and leaned away. "You've brought so much light into my life, sometimes it blinds me. You give and give and give. And three months ago, you gave me the greatest gift of all—our daughter. I love you, Abigail."

"I love you, too, Brady. You give me just as much as I give you—patience, and understanding, and love so tender, it takes my breath away."

After a gentle kiss on her forehead, Brady guided Abigail into the clearing, into the light. They walked toward Pine Hollow Lodge together, his arm around her shoulders, hers around his waist. Juliet cooed, birds chirped and the boughs whispered about Brady and Abigail's love, a love that would last forever.

* * * * *

Another wonderful year of romance
concludes with

Christmas
Memories

Share in the magic and memories of romance
during the holiday season with this collection of two
full-length contemporary Christmas stories,
by two bestselling authors

Diana Palmer
Marilyn Pappano

Available in December at your favorite retail outlet.

Only from 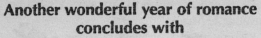 *Silhouette*®

where passion lives.

Silhouette

SPECIAL EDITION

™

THE BEST BRIDE
by Susan Mallery

HOMETOWN
HEARTBREAKERS

Hometown Heartbreakers: These heartstoppin' hunks
are rugged, ready and able to steal your heart....

Playing the field was what roguish Travis Haynes
did best—until he became a temporary family man.
Soon the unyielding lawman was weakened by a
little girl's touch—and completely undone by her
mother's kiss. But marriage-shy Elizabeth Abbott
wasn't about to become anyone's bride—
not even the oh-so-sexy Travis's!

Don't miss Susan Mallery's first book in her
Hometown Heartbreakers series, coming to you in
January...only from Silhouette Special Edition.

Silhouette

SPECIAL EDITION™

THE BLACKTHORN BROTHERHOOD
by Diana Whitney

Three men bound by a childhood secret are freed through family, friendship...and love.

Watch for the first book in Diana's Whitney's compelling new miniseries:

THE ADVENTURER
Special Edition #934, January 1995

Devon Monroe had finally come home, home to a haunting memory that made him want to keep running. Home to a woman who made him want to stand still and stare into her eyes. For there was something about Jessica Newcomb that made him forget about his own past and wonder long and hard about hers....

Look for THE AVENGER coming in the fall of 1995.

DWBB1

Silhouette

SPECIAL EDITION

™

The new year brings readers a powerful new trilogy—

This Time Forever

by Andrea Edwards

In January, don't miss A RING AND A PROMISE (SE #932).

Just one look at feisty Chicago caterer Kate Mallory made rancher
Jake MacNeill forget all about Montana. Could his lonesome-cowboy soul
rest as love overcomes unfulfilled promises of the past?

THIS TIME, FOREVER—sometimes a love is so strong, nothing can
stand in its way...not even time.

Look for the next installment, A ROSE AND A WEDDING VOW (SE #944),
in March 1995. Read along as two *old* friends learn that love is
worth taking a chance.

AEMINI-1

Montana Mavericks

Stories that capture living and loving
beneath the Big Sky, where legends live
on...and mystery lingers.

This December, explore more MONTANA MAVERICKS with

THE RANCHER TAKES A WIFE
by Jackie Merritt

He'd made up his mind. He'd loved her almost a lifetime
and now he was going to have her, come hell or high
water.

And don't miss a minute of the loving as the passion continues with:

OUTLAW LOVERS
by Pat Warren (January)

WAY OF THE WOLF
by Rebecca Daniels (February)

THE LAW IS NO LADY
by Helen R. Myers (March)
and many more!

Only from *Silhouette*® where passion lives.

SILHOUETTE... Where Passion Lives

Don't miss these Silhouette favorites by some of our most distinguished authors! And now you can receive a discount by ordering two or more titles!